THE CEO

© 2026 by Michael Whitworth

All rights reserved. No part of this publication may be reproduced, stored in a retrieval system, or transmitted in any form or by any means without the prior written permission of the author. The only exception is brief quotations in printed reviews.

ISBN 978-1-971767-01-7

Published by Start2Finish
Bend, Oregon 97702
start2finish.org

Printed in the United States of America

30 29 28 27 26   1 2 3 4 5

The CEO

A NOVEL

MICHAEL WHITWORTH

For my cousin Mary—

Your prayers, love, wisdom, and truth-telling have made a night-and-day difference in my life.

Contents

Chapter One	9
Chapter Two	13
Chapter Three	17
Chapter Four	21
Chapter Five	25
Chapter Six	29
Chapter Seven	35
Chapter Eight	39
Chapter Nine	45
Chapter Ten	49
Chapter Eleven	55
Chapter Twelve	61
Chapter Thirteen	65
Chapter Fourteen	71
Chapter Fifteen	77
Chapter Sixteen	87
Chapter Seventeen	93
Chapter Eighteen	99
Afterword	*107*

Chapter One

COMMENCEMENT

The word "commencement" means beginning. Adam Cole didn't think about that until years later, when he was old enough to understand that endings and beginnings are often the same door.

On the day he graduated from college, he sat on a folding chair in the middle of ten thousand other folding chairs, wearing a robe he would never wear again, and listened to a speech about changing the world. The speaker was a CEO—someone famous, someone whose company made something Adam couldn't remember now. The man said things like "dream big," "make your mark," and "the future is yours to write."

Adam believed him.

He was twenty-two years old. He had a business degree, a near-perfect GPA, and a sense that life was a ladder and he was ready to climb it. He didn't know yet that some ladders lean against the wrong wall. He didn't know that you can reach the top and find nothing there.

But that's getting ahead of the story.

That evening, after the ceremony, after the photographs with his parents, after the goodbye hugs with roommates who promised to stay in touch but wouldn't, Adam sat alone in his apartment. His suitcases were packed. His lease ended in three days. Everything he owned fit in the back of a used Honda Civic.

On the kitchen counter, two envelopes.

They had arrived on the same day, which seemed like a coincidence at the time. Two job offers, from two companies he'd interviewed with months ago. He'd almost forgotten about one of them.

The first envelope was heavy cream cardstock, embossed with a logo of a flame. *Fyre Inc.* He ran his thumb across the raised lettering. Even the paper felt expensive.

He opened it and read the terms, and his hands trembled slightly.

The salary was more than his father made in a year. The signing bonus alone could pay off his student loans. There was a company car—a BMW, the letter specified—and an apartment allowance in the city, and stock options that vested over five years, and a fast track to management for "high-potential candidates." The letter was signed personally by the CEO, a man named Lucian Fyre.

We see something special in you, Adam, the letter said. *You belong with us.*

Adam read those words three times. *You belong with us.* He had spent his whole life trying to belong somewhere. Trying to prove he was good enough. And here was proof, printed on paper so fine it almost glowed.

The second envelope was plain white and unremarkable. *Light Co.* He almost didn't open it.

The interview had been months ago, and it had been … different. No glass towers, no talk of market share or competitive advantage. Just a long conversation with a man named Joshua, who worked there and had asked Adam questions no interviewer had ever asked. *What kind of person do you want to become? What do you think you were made for?*

Adam hadn't known how to answer. He'd talked about career goals instead.

CHAPTER ONE

He opened the envelope anyway.

The salary was fair—comfortable, even—but not dazzling. The benefits were good. There was no signing bonus, no company car. The letter was brief, almost sparse.

We would be glad to have you, Adam, it said. *There is meaningful work here and a place at the table. But only you can decide if this is the path you want.*

It was signed by someone called "The Father." Adam thought that was strange—maybe the founder, maybe a nickname. Underneath, in smaller script, was a note in different handwriting: *The offer will remain open. —Joshua*

He set both letters on the counter and stared at them.

His phone buzzed. A text from Jake, his roommate, who had already left for his own job in another city: *Dude. Fyre Inc??? That's INSANE. You'd be crazy not to take it. Think of the parties. Think of the CAR.*

His phone buzzed again. His mother this time: *Thinking of you tonight, sweetheart. Such a big decision! No matter what you choose, Dad and I are proud of you. By the way—Mrs. Patterson's son works at that Light company. She says he just loves it there. Says they treat people like family. Just thought you should know. Call me when you decide. Love you.*

Adam turned off his phone.

The apartment was quiet. The streetlamp outside cast an orange glow through the window. He held the two letters, one in each hand, as if weighing them on a scale.

One felt like destiny. The other felt like … he wasn't sure. Something quieter. Something he couldn't name.

He thought about his father, who had worked the same job for thirty years and never complained. He thought about the CEO at graduation, talking about making a mark. He thought about the flame on the Fyre Inc. letterhead and how it seemed to flicker in the low light.

He didn't know it then, but this was the most important decision of his life. Not because of the money. Not because of the career. Because of who he would become.

Every road leads somewhere. The question is whether you'll recognize the destination before it's too late to turn back.

Adam stayed up until midnight, reading and rereading both letters. The Fyre Inc. offer never stopped glittering. The Light Co. offer never got louder. It just sat there, patient, like it had all the time in the world.

Finally, he turned off the lamp. He lay on his bare mattress—sheets already packed—and stared at the ceiling.

Tomorrow, he would decide.

Tomorrow, everything would begin.

Chapter Two

THE TOWER

The building was made of glass and ambition.

Adam stood on the sidewalk and looked up, shielding his eyes against the morning sun. Fyre Inc. headquarters rose forty stories into the sky, a spire of black glass that caught the light and threw it back like a challenge. All around him, men and women in expensive suits hurried past, coffee cups in hand, phones pressed to ears. They moved like people who mattered.

He wanted to be one of them.

The lobby was white marble and chrome, with ceilings so high they seemed to vanish. A waterfall cascaded down one wall—actual water, flowing over polished stone into a pool filled with black river rocks. The Fyre Inc. logo glowed behind the reception desk: a stylized flame, elegant and hypnotic.

Adam gave his name to the receptionist, a woman with perfect posture and a smile that didn't quite reach her eyes. She made a call, nodded, and gestured toward a bank of elevators.

"Someone will meet you on forty," she said.

The elevator rose so smoothly he barely felt it move. The doors opened onto a reception area with floor-to-ceiling windows and a view of the entire city. Adam could see the river, the bridges, the sprawl of buildings stretching to the horizon. From up here, everything looked small. Manageable. Conquerable.

"Adam Cole."

He turned. A man was walking toward him—not an assistant, not a junior executive. Adam recognized him from the company website, from magazine covers, from the signature on his offer letter.

Lucian Fyre.

He was taller than Adam expected, with silver hair swept back from a face that seemed ageless—not young, not old, just perfectly preserved. His suit was charcoal gray and impeccably tailored. His handshake was firm and warm.

"I wanted to welcome you personally," Lucian said. His voice was smooth, the kind of voice that made you lean in to listen. "We don't get many candidates like you, Adam. When I saw your file, I told my team—this one's special. This one's going places."

Adam felt heat rise to his face. "Thank you, sir. I—I'm honored."

"Lucian. Please." He smiled, and the smile was dazzling. "We're going to be colleagues. Let me show you around."

The tour lasted an hour. Lucian showed him everything: the trading floor, humming with energy and flashing screens; the executive dining room, where chefs prepared meals to order; the fitness center with its Olympic pool; the rooftop terrace where, Lucian mentioned casually, they sometimes landed helicopters.

"We take care of our people," Lucian said. "When you give everything to this company, the company gives everything back."

Adam nodded, trying to absorb it all. Everywhere he looked, there was more. More luxury, more technology, more proof that this was the center of something important.

They passed a cluster of employees in a glass-walled conference room, huddled over laptops. One of them—a young woman about Adam's age—looked up as they walked by. Her eyes met his for just a moment. She looked tired. Not just tired—hollowed out, like someone running on fumes. Then she looked back at her screen, and Adam looked away.

He told himself she was probably just having a long week.

"The thing about Fyre Inc.," Lucian was saying, "is that we're not just a company. We're a family. An elite family, yes—we don't accept just anyone—but once you're in, you're in. We protect our own."

They ended up in Lucian's office, a corner suite with windows on two sides. The desk was black lacquer. The chairs were leather. On the wall hung a single piece of art: a painting of a man holding a torch, leading others out of darkness.

Lucian gestured for Adam to sit.

"I'll be direct with you, Adam. I see myself in you. Twenty-five years ago, I was sitting where you're sitting—hungry, talented, ready to prove myself. Someone gave me a chance. Now I want to give you the same."

He leaned forward, and his eyes—gray, like the sky before a storm—locked onto Adam's.

"You could go somewhere else. Take a safer path. Settle for ordinary. But I don't think that's who you are." He paused. "Is it?"

Adam's heart was pounding. No one had ever spoken to him like this. No one had ever looked at him and seen… potential. Greatness. A future worth believing in.

"No, sir," he said. "It's not."

Lucian smiled. It was the smile of a man who had just won something.

"Good," he said. "Then let's talk about your future."

Adam left the building two hours later with a folder full of paperwork and a head full of dreams. The signing bonus had been increased. The apartment would be furnished. There was talk of a leadership development program, of mentorship, of a corner office within five years.

He stood on the sidewalk and looked up at the tower one more time. The sun had shifted, and the glass was darker now, more mirror than window. He could see his own reflection in it—small, distorted, swallowed by the building's shadow.

He didn't notice.

He was too busy imagining the view from the top.

There was still the other offer to consider—Light Co., with its quiet letter and its strange questions. He had scheduled a visit there for tomorrow. It seemed only fair to compare.

But standing in the shadow of Fyre Inc., with Lucian's words still ringing in his ears, Adam already knew. He had already decided. He just hadn't admitted it yet.

Some choices are made long before we sign anything. They're made in the moment we let ourselves want something more than we want the truth.

Adam wanted to matter. He wanted to be seen.

Lucian Fyre had seen him.

And that was enough.

Chapter Three

THE GARDEN

Light Co. was not what Adam expected.
The drive took him out of the city, past the financial district, past the suburbs, and into a stretch of countryside he didn't know existed so close to everything. The road wound through trees that were just beginning to bud with spring green. After twenty minutes, he almost turned back, sure he had the wrong address.
Then he saw it.
The building was old—a converted factory of red brick and tall windows, surrounded by lawns and walking paths and gardens that looked like someone actually tended them. No glass spire. No marble lobby. Just a simple sign by the entrance: *Light Co. Welcome.*
Adam parked his Honda next to a row of ordinary cars—Toyotas, Fords, a few bicycles chained to a rack—and walked toward the entrance. The air smelled like cut grass and something blooming. Birds were singing. It was so quiet he could hear his own footsteps on the gravel path.
He felt, unexpectedly, like he could breathe.
The front door was propped open. Inside, the lobby was warm wood and natural light, with plants on the windowsills

and a worn leather couch that looked like people actually sat on it. A woman at the front desk smiled when she saw him—a real smile, the kind that crinkled her eyes.

"You must be Adam," she said. "Joshua's expecting you. He'll be right down."

Adam nodded, unsure what to do with himself. There was no waterfall, no chrome, no logo glowing on the wall. Just a small framed quote near the door, handwritten in simple script: *We are his workmanship.*

He didn't recognize the words, but something about them stayed with him.

Joshua appeared a few minutes later, coming down a staircase with the easy stride of someone who wasn't in a hurry. He was younger than Adam remembered—early thirties, maybe—with dark hair and a face that was hard to place. Not handsome in the way Lucian Fyre was handsome. Just... open. Like he had nothing to hide.

"Adam." Joshua extended his hand. His grip was firm but unhurried. "I'm glad you came."

"Thanks for having me," Adam said. He glanced around. "This place is ... different."

Joshua smiled. "Different than what?"

Adam hesitated. He didn't want to mention Fyre Inc., but Joshua seemed to understand anyway.

"Come on," Joshua said. "Let me show you around."

They walked through the building together. Joshua pointed out the workspaces—open rooms with good light, where people sat at desks or gathered in clusters, talking. Some waved as they passed. One man was laughing at something on his screen. A woman was eating lunch at her desk, reading a paperback novel.

No one looked exhausted. No one looked hollowed out.

"What exactly does Light Co. do?" Adam asked.

Joshua thought about it. "We help people," he said. "Different ways, depending on the need. Consulting. Development.

CHAPTER THREE

Sometimes we just ... fix things that are broken." He glanced at Adam. "The work matters. That's the point."

It was a vague answer. At Fyre Inc., Lucian had talked about market share and growth projections and industry disruption. This felt ... smaller. Quieter.

Adam wasn't sure if that was a good thing or not.

They ended up outside, on a bench near a small pond. Ducks floated on the water. The afternoon sun was warm on Adam's face.

"Can I ask you something?" Joshua said.

"Sure."

"What do you want your life to be about?"

Adam blinked. It wasn't the kind of question he was used to. Interviewers asked about his five-year plan. His strengths and weaknesses. His salary expectations. No one asked what his life should be *about*.

"I want to be successful," he said.

Joshua nodded slowly. "What does that mean to you?"

Adam opened his mouth, then closed it. He thought of the glass tower, the corner office, the BMW, the view from the fortieth floor. He thought of Lucian saying, *You belong with us.*

"I guess ... I want to matter," he said finally. "I want to do something that counts. Be someone people respect."

Joshua was quiet for a moment. A duck dove under the water and came up with something in its beak.

"There are different kinds of mattering," Joshua said. "There's the kind where people know your name. And there's the kind where you become the person you were meant to be." He looked at Adam. "They're not always the same thing."

Adam didn't know what to say. The words felt true, but he couldn't hold onto them. They were like water slipping through his fingers.

They walked back to the lobby together. At the door, Joshua handed Adam a folder—much thinner than the one from Fyre Inc.

"The offer's in there," Joshua said. "Take your time. There's no pressure, no deadline. If it's right for you, you'll know."

Adam tucked the folder under his arm. "And if I choose ... somewhere else?"

Joshua smiled—not a salesman's smile, not a winning smile, just a smile. "Then the offer stays open. For whenever you're ready."

Adam frowned. "That doesn't make business sense."

"Maybe not." Joshua shrugged. "But it's how we do things. My Father's patient."

There it was again—*the Father*. Adam wanted to ask who that was, but something stopped him. Maybe he wasn't ready to know.

He shook Joshua's hand and walked to his car. Before he got in, he looked back at the old factory with its brick walls and its gardens and its simple sign. People were leaving for the day, saying goodbye to each other, laughing about something. One man had his arm around his colleague's shoulder.

It looked like a good place to work.

But it didn't look like the future Adam had imagined. It didn't look like greatness. It looked ... ordinary.

He drove back to the city with the windows down, thinking about Joshua's question. *What do you want your life to be about?*

He still didn't have an answer. Or maybe he did, and it just wasn't the right one.

Years later, he would remember this drive. He would remember the sunlight through the trees, and the smell of the gardens, and the way Joshua had looked at him—not like a prospect to be closed, but like a person worth waiting for.

He would remember the fork in the road and the path he didn't take.

And he would be grateful, more than he could say, that the offer had remained open.

Chapter Four

THE SIGNATURE

Adam spent two days pretending he hadn't already decided. He made lists. Pros and cons, written on a yellow legal pad in his empty apartment. He called his father, who listened quietly and said, "Seems like either one would be fine, son. What does your gut tell you?" He called his mother, who said, "I just want you to be happy. Really happy, not just successful-happy. You know the difference."

He didn't know the difference. Not yet.

He texted Jake a photo of both offer letters, side by side. Jake's response came in seconds: *Bro. This isn't even a question. Fyre Inc is the dream. Light Co sounds like a nonprofit for hippies.*

Adam laughed. Jake was always like that—certain, confident, untroubled by ambiguity. It must be nice, Adam thought, to see the world in such clean lines.

He looked at his pro-con list. The Fyre Inc. column was full of tangible things: salary, signing bonus, car, apartment, stock options, prestige, networking, corner office. The Light Co. column had vaguer entries: *seemed peaceful, people looked happy, Joshua asked good questions, offer stays open.*

How do you weigh peace against a BMW?

He told himself it wasn't really a choice. It was just math.

THE CEO

On the third morning, Adam woke early. His lease was up in six hours. His car was packed. It was time to decide, or time to admit he already had.

He sat at the kitchen counter with the Fyre Inc. paperwork spread in front of him. The contract was thick—forty pages of legalese, clauses about non-compete agreements and intellectual property and stock vesting schedules. He didn't read most of it. He was twenty-two years old, and he trusted that a company this impressive wouldn't do anything unfair.

Besides, he told himself, it wasn't permanent. He could always leave later. Work there a few years, pay off his loans, build his résumé, and then reassess. People did that all the time.

He didn't know yet how chains work. How they start as bracelets.

He picked up the pen. It was heavy and silver—a gift from his parents for graduation, engraved with his initials. He turned to the signature page. There was a line waiting for him, and below it, in small print: *By signing, I agree to the terms and conditions outlined in this agreement.*

He thought of Joshua asking, *What do you want your life to be about?*

He thought of Lucian saying, *You belong with us.*

He signed.

The moment the pen left the paper, something shifted. It was small—just a tightness in his chest, a flicker of something that might have been doubt or might have been fear. He told himself it was excitement. The nervousness of beginning something big.

He initialed the other pages quickly, not reading them, and slid the contract into the prepaid envelope Fyre Inc. had provided. It was done. He was theirs.

Now there was only one thing left to do.

The phone rang three times before Joshua answered.

"Adam." His voice was warm, unhurried, like he'd been expecting the call. "How are you?"

CHAPTER FOUR

"I'm good," Adam said. He was pacing his empty living room, footsteps echoing on the bare floor. "I wanted to call and ... well, thank you. For the offer. For taking the time to meet with me."

"Of course."

Adam took a breath. "I've decided to go another direction. I'm going to take a position at ... at another company. I wanted to let you know personally."

There was a pause. Not a long one, but enough for Adam to wonder what Joshua was thinking. Disappointment? Judgment? The salesman's pivot to a hard close?

"I understand," Joshua said. His voice hadn't changed. No guilt, no pressure, no edge. "I appreciate you calling."

Adam exhaled. "You're not going to try to change my mind?"

Joshua laughed softly. "Would it work?"

Adam thought about the signed contract in the envelope, the BMW waiting for him, and the corner office in five years. "Probably not," he admitted.

"Then I won't try." There was kindness in Joshua's voice, and something else—something that sounded almost like sorrow. "But Adam, I want you to remember something."

"What?"

"The offer will remain open."

Adam frowned. "You said that before. I don't understand. What if you fill the position?"

"There's always a place for you here, Adam. That's not a position—that's a promise." Joshua paused. "Whenever you're ready. If things don't work out the way you hope. If you find yourself ... lost. Just call. I'll come find you."

Adam didn't know what to say. The words were strange—too generous, too certain. No company made promises like that. No one waited for someone who'd already said no.

"Thanks," he managed. "I appreciate that."

"Take care of yourself, Adam."

The line went quiet. Adam stood there for a long moment, phone in hand, staring at the wall.

Then he picked up the envelope with the signed contract, walked outside, and dropped it in the mailbox.

He drove to the city that afternoon. The furnished apartment Fyre Inc. had arranged was on the thirty-second floor of a sleek high-rise, all floor-to-ceiling windows and modern furniture and a view that made the world look small. The keys were waiting for him at the front desk, along with a welcome basket: champagne, chocolates, and a card signed by Lucian Fyre himself.

Welcome to the family, the card said. *Your future starts now.*

Adam popped the champagne. He drank a glass alone, watching the sun set over the skyline. His phone buzzed with congratulations from Jake, from college friends, from people he barely remembered adding on social media. Everyone was impressed. Everyone said he'd made it.

He called his mother to tell her the news. She was quiet for a moment, then said, "I'm proud of you, sweetheart. Just ... don't forget who you are. Okay?"

"I won't, Mom."

But he would. That's exactly what would happen. Slowly, piece by piece, he would forget who he was. He would become someone else—someone harder, hollower, more successful, and less alive.

He didn't know that yet, standing at the window with champagne in his hand.

All he knew was that he'd made it. He was here. The future was his.

Far below, the city glittered like a promise. Far above, the glass tower of Fyre Inc. caught the last light of the day and held it, burning, until the sun disappeared and everything went dark.

Chapter Five

ORIENTATION

The first week was a dream.

Adam arrived at Fyre Inc. on a Monday morning, and from the moment he stepped through the glass doors, he felt like he'd entered another world. The new employee orientation was held in a penthouse conference room with catered breakfast—fresh fruit, artisan pastries, and coffee that cost more per cup than Adam used to spend on dinner. There were twelve new hires, all young, all bright-eyed, all chosen.

A senior HR executive welcomed them with a speech about excellence. "You are the top one percent," she said. "We don't hire good. We hire extraordinary. Look around this room. These are your peers now. These are the people who will change the world with you."

Adam looked around. The others were nodding, sitting up straighter, trying to look like the extraordinary people they'd just been told they were. He felt it too—that rush of belonging, of being selected, of finally arriving somewhere that matched his ambition.

They were given laptops, company phones, and keycards that opened every door. They were shown the gym, the cafeteria, the meditation room, the nap pods. "We believe in taking care of our people," the HR executive said. "When you give your best, we give our best back."

No one mentioned that giving your best meant giving everything. That would come later.

Adam was assigned to the Strategic Development division, which sounded important, even though he wasn't entirely sure what it meant. His desk was on the thirty-eighth floor, two levels below Lucian's office, with a view of the river. The chair was ergonomic. The monitor was enormous. On his first day, there was a welcome gift waiting: a leather portfolio embossed with his initials, a Montblanc pen, and a note that said, *Great things ahead. —L.F.*

He texted a photo to Jake: *Day one.*

Jake's reply: *You absolute legend.*

His manager was a woman named Claire, sharp and polished, who spoke in bullet points and scheduled meetings in fifteen-minute increments. She assigned him to a high-profile project almost immediately—a market analysis for a major client. "We don't ease people in here," she said. "Sink or swim. That's how we find out what you're made of."

Adam swam. He stayed late every night that first week, learning the systems, studying the data, trying to prove he belonged. The work was demanding but exhilarating. He felt like an athlete finally playing in the big leagues.

On Thursday, Lucian Fyre stopped by his desk.

Adam didn't even see him coming—just looked up, and there he was, silver hair immaculate, that warm predator's smile on his face.

"How's our rising star?" Lucian asked.

Adam stood up so fast he almost knocked over his coffee. "Mr. Fyre. I—I'm doing great. Learning a lot."

"Lucian." The CEO put a hand on Adam's shoulder. "I've heard good things. Claire says you're a natural. Keep it up. I'm watching."

He was gone before Adam could respond, gliding down

the hallway like a shark through still water. But Adam stood there for a full minute afterward, heart pounding, replaying the words. *I'm watching.* It felt like a blessing. Like being anointed.

He didn't notice that the colleague at the next desk had flinched when Lucian walked by. He didn't see the way she kept her eyes fixed on her screen, barely breathing, until the CEO was gone.

On Friday evening, Adam was still at his desk at eight o'clock, reviewing spreadsheets, when a voice interrupted him.

"You're the new kid. Cole, right?"

He looked up. A man stood in the doorway of a corner office—mid-forties, fit, with graying temples and a suit that probably cost more than Adam's car. His smile was easy, practiced, the smile of someone who'd learned to wear success like a comfortable coat.

"Adam Cole," Adam said, standing. "And you're…"

"Marcus Webb. Senior VP, Strategic Development." He walked over and shook Adam's hand. "Which means I'm your boss' boss. Don't worry—I don't bite. Unless you miss a deadline."

Adam laughed, a little nervously. "I'll keep that in mind."

Marcus leaned against the cubicle wall, studying him. "Lucian's taken a shine to you. That's rare. He doesn't notice most new hires until they've been here a year."

"I got lucky, I guess."

"Luck." Marcus' smile flickered, just for a moment. "Sure. Let's call it that."

He straightened up and glanced out the window at the darkening city. "Listen, Adam. You seem like a sharp kid. Driven. Hungry. That's good—you'll need it here. But let me give you some advice."

"Of course."

Marcus looked at him, and for just a second, something passed across his face. Something tired. Something almost like a warning.

"Enjoy the honeymoon phase," he said quietly. "It doesn't last."

Before Adam could ask what he meant, Marcus' phone buzzed. He checked it, and the easy smile returned, sliding into place like a mask.

"Duty calls. Get some rest this weekend—you've earned it. And welcome to the family."

He walked back toward his corner office, and Adam watched him go. The phrase echoed: *Welcome to the family.* Lucian had said the same thing. So had the welcome card. It was everywhere, that word. *Family.*

Adam gathered his things and headed for the elevator. The building was quiet now, most of the lights dimmed, but he could see a few offices still glowing. People hunched over computers. People who'd been there when he arrived at eight that morning and were still there now, twelve hours later.

He told himself that was dedication. Passion. The price of excellence.

He didn't ask what Marcus had meant by "honeymoon phase." He didn't want to know.

Not yet.

Chapter Six

PROMOTION

Six months in, Adam got the call.

Claire asked him to come to her office at four o'clock. When he arrived, she was smiling—a real smile, not the clipped professional one she usually wore. Marcus Webb was there too, standing by the window.

"Close the door," Claire said.

Adam's heart was pounding as he sat down. He'd been working seventy-hour weeks, sometimes more. He'd delivered three major projects ahead of schedule. He'd earned this—whatever this was.

"We're promoting you," Claire said. "Senior Associate, effective immediately. New title, new salary, new office. Congratulations."

Adam exhaled. Six months. Most people waited two years for this. He thought of his father, who'd worked the same job for three decades without a single promotion, and he felt a swell of something that might have been pride or might have been distance.

"You've earned it," Marcus said from the window. "Lucian's impressed. That doesn't happen often."

That night, there was a dinner in the executive dining

room. White tablecloths, waiters in black, and a toast from Lucian himself. He stood at the head of the table with a glass of wine raised and said, "To Adam Cole. He understands what it takes. He's one of us now."

Everyone clapped. Adam felt the warmth of it wash over him—the attention, the approval, the sense that he had finally, finally arrived.

He didn't notice that Marcus barely touched his wine. He didn't see the way Marcus watched Lucian with something careful in his eyes, something guarded.

Adam was too busy glowing.

The promotion came with a new office—glass walls, a view of the river, and his name on the door. It also came with new expectations. The seventy-hour weeks became eighty. The projects multiplied. Adam started carrying two phones: one for work and one for everything else. The work phone never stopped buzzing.

He told himself it was temporary. Just until he proved himself at this new level. Just until things settled down.

Things never settled down.

His father's birthday fell on a Saturday in October. Adam had planned to drive home for the weekend—his mother had called three times to confirm, and his father, who never asked for anything, had mentioned he was looking forward to it.

On Friday afternoon, Claire dropped a folder on his desk. "Major client dinner tomorrow night. Lucian specifically asked for you to be there. It's a big opportunity."

Adam stared at the folder. "Tomorrow? I have—I was supposed to—"

Claire was already walking away. "Seven o'clock. Don't be late."

He sat there for a long time, looking at the folder. Then he picked up his personal phone and called his mother.

"Hey, Mom. Listen … something came up at work. I'm not going to be able to make it this weekend."

CHAPTER SIX

Silence. Then: "Oh. Okay, sweetheart. Your father will understand."

But her voice said something different. Her voice said he wouldn't understand, not really, and neither did she.

"I'll make it up to him," Adam said. "I promise. Next month."

"Sure. Next month."

Next month never came. There was always another dinner, another deadline, another opportunity too important to miss. Adam sent a gift—an expensive watch, nicer than anything his father had ever owned—and told himself it was enough.

His father called to thank him. "It's a beautiful watch, son. I'll wear it every day."

He didn't say what Adam knew he was thinking: *I'd rather have you.*

Emily broke up with him in November.

She'd been his girlfriend since junior year of college—smart, patient, and kind. She'd moved to the city to be near him, taken a job at a nonprofit, and waited for him on the nights he came home late, which was every night.

They were supposed to have dinner on a Tuesday. Adam canceled—a last-minute crisis at work. They rescheduled for Thursday. He canceled again. On Saturday, he promised he'd be there, and he meant it, but then Lucian called personally to ask him to review a presentation, and what was he supposed to say?

Emily was sitting on his couch when he got home at eleven. Her eyes were red.

"I can't do this anymore," she said.

Adam set down his briefcase. "Em, I'm sorry. I know I've been busy, but things will slow down soon. I just need to—"

"You always say that." Her voice cracked. "Things will slow down. Next month. After this project. But they never do, Adam. They never do, and I'm tired of being something you fit in between meetings."

He wanted to argue. He wanted to tell her she didn't understand the pressure he was under, the stakes, the opportunity. But he looked at her—really looked at her—and saw something he hadn't seen before. She was grieving. Not for the relationship, but for him. For the person he used to be.

"I don't even know who you are anymore," she said quietly. "And I don't think you do either."

She left that night. Adam stood at the window of his thirty-second-floor apartment, watching the city lights blur through something that might have been exhaustion or might have been tears.

He told himself it was for the best. She didn't fit into his life anymore. She wanted something small and ordinary, and he was building something bigger.

He told himself a lot of things that year.

At the company Christmas party, Lucian gave a speech. He talked about record profits, about market dominance, and about the family they'd built together. Then he pointed at Adam, standing near the back with a glass of champagne he didn't want.

"Adam Cole," Lucian said. "Stand up. Let everyone see you."

Adam stood, face flushing.

"This young man has been with us less than a year, and already he's outperforming people who've been here a decade. That's what we're about. That's the Fyre Inc. way. Talent. Drive. Sacrifice." Lucian raised his glass. "To Adam. And to everyone willing to give everything for this family."

Everyone drank. Everyone applauded. Adam smiled and nodded and felt the heat of all those eyes on him.

Later, in the bathroom, he looked at himself in the mirror. He barely recognized the man looking back. The face was thinner, the eyes harder, the jaw set in a way that hadn't been there before.

"I don't even know who you are anymore," Emily had said.

CHAPTER SIX

He splashed water on his face and went back to the party. There was networking to do, hands to shake, and a future to build.

The cost of that future was becoming clearer every day. But Adam wasn't counting anymore.

He'd already paid too much to stop.

Chapter Seven

COMPROMISE

The first time Adam lied for Fyre Inc., he told himself it wasn't really lying.

It was March of his second year. He was leading a team now, four analysts who reported to him, and they'd been working on a market projection for a major acquisition. The numbers were good—solid growth, reasonable risk—but they weren't spectacular. And Lucian wanted spectacular.

The request came through Claire, delivered casually, almost as an afterthought. "Lucian reviewed the projections. He thinks we should revisit the growth assumptions. Maybe adjust them upward. Ten, fifteen percent."

Adam frowned at the spreadsheet on his screen. "The data doesn't support that. We'd be overstating the potential."

"We'd be presenting an optimistic scenario." Claire's voice was smooth, unbothered. "That's not the same thing. Clients expect a range of outcomes. We're just ... emphasizing the upside."

"By changing the numbers."

"By adjusting the assumptions." She tilted her head. "Adam, this is how things work. Every firm does it. We're not fabricating data—we're interpreting it favorably. There's a difference."

He wanted to argue. He wanted to say that a lie dressed in a suit was still a lie, that "adjusting assumptions" was just a polite word for deception. But Claire was already moving toward the door, and the implication was clear: this wasn't a discussion. It was an instruction.

"Lucian's counting on you," she said over her shoulder. "Don't let him down."

Adam sat at his desk for a long time after she left, staring at the spreadsheet.

He thought about his father, who had worked the same honest job for thirty years. He thought about his mother, who had taught Sunday school and always said that integrity was what you did when no one was watching. He thought about the ethics course he'd taken in college, where everything had seemed so clear, so black and white.

But that was before. Before the corner office and the company car. Before the stock options that would vest in three more years. Before he'd built a life that depended on staying exactly where he was.

He pulled up the projection model and looked at the assumptions. Growth rate: 8%. That was what the data supported. That was the truth.

His fingers hovered over the keyboard.

Everyone does it, Claire had said. Maybe she was right. Maybe this was just how the game was played. Maybe his college ethics professor had never worked in the real world, never faced a choice between his principles and his career.

He changed the number. 8% became 12%.

It was a small change. Four percentage points. Hardly anything, really. The projection still fell within a plausible range. It wasn't fraud—it was optimism. It was telling the client what they wanted to hear.

He saved the file and sent it to Claire.

That night, he couldn't sleep.

He lay in bed, staring at the ceiling of his expensive

CHAPTER SEVEN

apartment, listening to the hum of the city below. The number kept flashing in his mind. 8%. 12%. Such a small difference. Such a small betrayal.

But something had shifted. He could feel it—a crack in something that used to be solid, a line that used to be clear. He had always thought of himself as honest. He had always believed that when the moment came, he would do the right thing.

The moment had come. And he hadn't.

He told himself it was just once. A one-time thing, a necessary compromise to keep the peace. He wouldn't do it again. Next time, he'd push back. Next time, he'd stand his ground.

But next time came sooner than he expected. And the time after that. And the time after that.

Each compromise was small. Each one could be justified, explained, rationalized. A generous interpretation here. An omitted detail there. A number rounded up instead of down. None of it was illegal—not technically—and everyone was doing it, and what difference did one analyst make in the grand scheme of things?

The difference, Adam would learn, was in what it did to him.

Each small lie made the next one easier. Each crossed line moved the boundary a little further. He was like a man walking into the ocean, one step at a time, telling himself the water wasn't that deep—until the day he looked back and couldn't see the shore.

A few weeks later, he ran into Marcus Webb in the elevator.

It was late—past ten—and they were both heading down. Marcus looked tired, his tie loosened, his jacket slung over one arm. For a moment, neither of them spoke.

Then Marcus said, quietly, "You adjusted the Hendricks projection."

Adam's stomach dropped. "I—yes. Claire asked me to revisit the assumptions."

"Claire." Marcus smiled, but there was no humor in it. "Right. Claire asked."

The elevator descended in silence. Adam watched the numbers tick down and felt the weight of Marcus' gaze.

"Let me tell you something, Adam." Marcus' voice was low, almost gentle. "I've been here fifteen years. I've seen a lot of people come through. Bright kids, like you. Hungry. Talented. Most of them adjust those numbers when they're asked."

"And the ones who don't?"

Marcus looked at him. His eyes were tired—not just from the late night, but from something deeper. Something years in the making.

"They leave. Or they're pushed out. And the ones who stay…" He paused. "The ones who stay become like me."

The elevator doors opened. The lobby was empty, the lights dimmed. Marcus stepped out, then turned back.

"I used to be like you," he said. "I used to think I could play the game without becoming it. Keep a little piece of myself separate, untouched." He shook his head slowly. "You can't. The game doesn't work that way."

Adam stood frozen in the elevator doorway. "Then why do you stay?"

Marcus smiled that tired, humorless smile again.

"Because I've been here fifteen years," he said. "And I don't know who I am without it anymore."

He walked away into the night, and Adam watched him go.

The elevator doors began to close. Adam stepped out just in time, his heart pounding, Marcus' words echoing in his head.

I don't know who I am without it anymore.

He told himself that would never be him. He told himself he was different, smarter, more self-aware. He would know when to stop. He would know when he'd gone too far.

But that's the thing about going too far. You never know you've done it until you try to turn around and find that you can't.

Chapter Eight

THE HANDCUFFS

By his second anniversary at Fyre Inc., Adam had everything he'd ever wanted.

He had the corner office with the floor-to-ceiling windows. He had the title—Director of Strategic Development, the youngest in company history. He had the salary, the bonus structure, the stock options that would be worth a small fortune if he stayed three more years. He had the respect of his peers, the attention of leadership, the golden glow of someone marked for greatness.

He also had a prescription for Xanax that he refilled every month. He had a bottle of whiskey in his desk drawer that he told himself was for clients. He had a recurring nightmare where the walls of his office turned to glass and everyone could see him drowning.

He had everything. And he was miserable.

The panic attacks started in the fall.

The first one hit during a board presentation. Adam was standing at the front of the room, clicking through slides, when suddenly his chest tightened and he couldn't breathe. The room tilted. His vision narrowed to a tunnel. He gripped the podium and forced himself to keep talking, the words coming out mechanical and strange, while inside he was certain he was dying.

Afterward, in the bathroom, he splashed water on his face and stared at his reflection. His skin was gray. His hands were shaking. He looked like a man who'd seen a ghost.

Maybe he had. Maybe the ghost was himself.

The attacks came more frequently after that. In meetings. On calls. Once, in the middle of the night, jolting him awake with the certainty that something was terribly wrong. He went to a doctor, who ran tests and found nothing physically wrong. "Stress," the doctor said. "You need to slow down."

Slow down. As if that were an option. As if he could walk into Lucian's office and say, "I need to take it easy for a while." He would be replaced within a week. Someone younger, hungrier, more willing to bleed.

So he took the Xanax and kept going.

The drinking came next.

It started innocently enough—a glass of wine with dinner to unwind, a nightcap to help him sleep. But dinner kept getting later, and the nightcap turned into two, then three, and soon Adam couldn't imagine going to bed without the warm blur of alcohol softening the edges of his thoughts.

He wasn't an alcoholic. He told himself that every morning, nursing a headache and a cup of black coffee. Alcoholics couldn't function, and he was functioning fine. Better than fine. He was excelling. The performance reviews said so.

But some nights, alone in his apartment with the city glittering thirty-two stories below, he would pour a drink and stand at the window and feel absolutely nothing. Not happy, not sad, not anxious—just empty. A hollow man in a beautiful shell, going through the motions of a life he no longer recognized as his own.

He stopped calling his mother. The conversations had become too painful—her gentle questions, his evasive answers, and the silences that said more than words. She knew something was wrong. She always knew. And he couldn't bear to hear the worry in her voice when he had nothing to offer but lies.

"I'm fine, Mom. Just busy. You know how it is."

She didn't know how it was. She had never sold pieces of her soul for a corner office.

One night, Adam ran the numbers on what it would cost to leave.

He sat at his kitchen table with his contract spread out in front of him, highlighter in hand, reading the fine print he'd never bothered to read before. The signing bonus he'd spent on furniture and student loans—that had a clawback clause. If he left before three years, he owed it back. All of it. The stock options—those didn't vest for another two years. If he walked away now, they were worthless. The relocation package, the apartment subsidy, the company car—all of it had strings attached, penalties for early departure, hooks buried in the legalese.

And then there was the non-compete. Two years. He couldn't work for any competitor, any client, any company in the same industry. Two years of unemployment, essentially, if he wanted to leave.

Adam stared at the numbers. He had climbed into a gilded cage and locked the door behind him, and he hadn't even noticed until now.

He thought about people who left anyway. He'd seen it happen—a senior manager who'd resigned last year to take care of a sick parent. Within a month, Lucian had made calls. References were poisoned. Job offers evaporated. The woman ended up moving to another city, starting over from nothing, her reputation in ashes.

"We take care of our family," Lucian always said. What he didn't say was the other half of that sentence: *And we destroy anyone who tries to leave.*

Adam poured another drink and laughed—a hollow, bitter sound that echoed in the empty apartment. He'd thought he was building a career. He'd been building a prison.

He ran into Marcus in the parking garage a few days later. It was late—nearly midnight—and they were both heading to their cars.

"You look terrible," Marcus said. It wasn't unkind, just honest.

"Thanks." Adam managed a tired smile. "You really know how to cheer a guy up."

Marcus leaned against his car, studying him. "How long since you've slept? Really slept?"

Adam thought about it. He couldn't remember. The nights blurred together—the Xanax, the whiskey, the restless half-sleep filled with dreams of drowning.

"I'm fine," he said.

"No, you're not." Marcus' voice was quiet. "You're where I was, ten years ago. Running on fumes and telling yourself it's fuel."

Adam felt something crack open inside him—something he'd been holding shut for months. "I can't leave," he said. His voice came out rough, almost a whisper. "I looked at the contract. The non-compete, the clawbacks—I'm trapped. I can't afford to go, and I can't afford to stay, and I don't know what to do."

Marcus was silent for a long moment. The garage was empty, their voices echoing off the concrete.

"The cage looks golden from the outside," Marcus said finally. "But it's still a cage." He shook his head. "I wish I had answers for you, Adam. I really do. But I've been looking for a way out for fifteen years, and I still haven't found one."

He got into his car and drove away, leaving Adam alone in the garage.

Adam stood there for a long time, under the fluorescent lights, listening to the silence. He thought about the boy he'd been two years ago—hopeful, ambitious, certain that success would make him happy. He thought about the man he'd become—hollow, anxious, successful by every metric except the ones that mattered.

CHAPTER EIGHT

He thought about Joshua's voice on the phone, so long ago it felt like another lifetime: *The offer will remain open.*

He almost laughed. What good was an open offer when you couldn't walk through the door?

He got in his car and drove home to his empty apartment, his expensive whiskey, and his dreamless pharmaceutical sleep.

He didn't know it yet, but he was almost at the bottom.

And sometimes, the bottom is where grace finds you.

Chapter Nine

THE ABYSS

The day Adam hit bottom started like any other.
He was in his office by seven, coffee in hand, reviewing a presentation for a ten o'clock meeting. The project was a major acquisition—months of work, dozens of people involved. Adam had overseen the financial modeling. His team had done the analysis.
His team. That included Daniel Chen.
Daniel was twenty-five, two years out of business school, eager and earnest in a way that reminded Adam of himself—the self he used to be, before. They'd become something like friends over the past year, as much as anyone at Fyre Inc. could be friends. Daniel brought Adam coffee when he forgot to eat. Adam helped Daniel navigate the politics of the office. It wasn't much, but in a place like this, it meant something.
Three weeks ago, Adam had found an error in Daniel's calculations. A significant one—a decimal point in the wrong place that cascaded through the entire model. It changed the projected returns by nearly twenty percent.
Adam had fixed it. Quietly, late at night, when no one else was around. He'd corrected the number and said nothing to Daniel, nothing to anyone. Better to let it disappear. Better to protect them both.

But he'd missed something. A linked cell in another spreadsheet. A backup file that hadn't been updated. Somewhere in the maze of documents, the wrong number survived.

And now it was ten o'clock, and Lucian was standing at the front of the boardroom, and everything was about to fall apart.

The client's CFO found it on slide thirty-seven.

"Wait," she said, frowning at her printed copy. "This number doesn't match your earlier projection. You've got eighteen percent here, but page twelve says twenty-two percent."

The room went quiet. Lucian's smile froze. Adam felt the blood drain from his face.

The next twenty minutes were chaos. Questions, recriminations, frantic page-flipping. The error was obvious once you saw it—a fundamental inconsistency that made the entire analysis unreliable. The client excused herself to make a phone call. Lucian excused everyone except his senior team.

Adam stood against the wall, heart pounding, as Lucian turned to face them. The CEO's eyes were cold—colder than Adam had ever seen them.

"Who is responsible for the financial model?"

Claire cleared her throat. "Adam's team handled the analysis. Daniel Chen was the primary analyst."

Lucian's gaze shifted to Adam. "Is that correct?"

Adam's mouth went dry. He thought about Daniel—young, hardworking Daniel, who trusted him, who looked up to him. He thought about the error he'd found and fixed, the error he'd never reported. If he spoke now, if he explained what had happened, they would both go down. Two careers destroyed instead of one.

But if he stayed silent...

"Yes," Adam heard himself say. "Daniel was the primary analyst."

The words came out steady and professional. The words of a man protecting himself. The words of a coward.

Lucian nodded. "Have him cleared out by end of day."

CHAPTER NINE

Adam didn't see it happen. He couldn't bring himself to watch.

He stayed in his office with the door closed, pretending to work, while security escorted Daniel out of the building. He heard the whispers in the hallway, the murmured shock of colleagues. He heard the elevator ding as Daniel left—left with a cardboard box and a ruined career and no idea that the man who could have saved him had chosen not to.

At five o'clock, Adam's phone buzzed. A text from Daniel: *I don't know what happened. I checked that model a hundred times. I'm so sorry, Adam. I hope this doesn't reflect badly on you.*

Adam stared at the words. Daniel was apologizing to *him*. Daniel, who had just lost everything, was worried about *Adam's* reputation.

Something inside Adam cracked. Not a small crack this time—a fissure, deep and widening, splitting him open.

He didn't reply. He couldn't. What would he say? *I'm sorry I destroyed your career to save mine? I'm sorry I'm too much of a coward to tell the truth?*

He turned off his phone, put on his coat, and walked to the parking garage.

He sat in his car for two hours.

He didn't turn on the engine. He didn't turn on the radio. He just sat there, hands on the steering wheel, staring at the concrete wall in front of him.

He thought about every choice that had led him here. The offer he'd accepted. The compromises he'd made. The lies he'd told—to clients, to colleagues, to himself. Each one had seemed small at the time, justified, necessary. But they'd added up, brick by brick, until he'd built a prison around his own soul.

And now this. A man's career—a man's *life*—sacrificed so Adam could keep his corner office and his stock options and his slow, comfortable descent into damnation.

He looked at his reflection in the rearview mirror. The face that looked back was a stranger's—gaunt, gray, hollow-eyed. A dead man who hadn't stopped breathing yet.

You were dead in your trespasses and sins.

The words surfaced from somewhere deep—a Sunday school class, a sermon half-remembered, his mother's voice reading Scripture at the kitchen table. He hadn't thought about God in years. He'd been too busy building his kingdom to think about anyone else's.

But sitting in that parking garage, in the fluorescent darkness, he felt the weight of those words like a stone on his chest. Dead. He was dead. Successful, respected, powerful—and dead. Walking through life as a corpse in a tailored suit.

He wanted to pray. He tried to pray. But the words wouldn't come. He'd forgotten how. Or maybe he'd never really known—maybe his faith had always been secondhand, borrowed from his mother, never truly his own.

All he could manage was a single word, whispered into the silence of the car:

"Help."

It wasn't much of a prayer. It wasn't eloquent or theological or even particularly faithful. It was the groan of a man drowning, reaching for anything that might save him.

He didn't know if anyone was listening.

He didn't know if he deserved to be heard.

But somewhere, far away and closer than breath, Someone was. And Someone had been waiting—patiently, faithfully—for exactly this moment.

The offer was still open.

It had never closed.

Chapter Ten

THE ENCOUNTER

Three days after Daniel was fired, Adam found himself on the loading dock.

He wasn't sure how he'd gotten there. He had a vague memory of leaving his office, walking past the elevators, and pushing through a door marked *Employees Only*. The loading dock was at the back of the building, a concrete platform where delivery trucks came and went. No one from the executive floors ever came down here. That was the point.

He sat on a stack of wooden pallets, his tie loosened, his jacket abandoned somewhere upstairs. The afternoon sun was warm on his face, but he couldn't feel it. He couldn't feel much of anything anymore.

He'd missed two meetings today. Claire had called three times. He'd let it go to voicemail. What was the point? What was the point of any of it?

He thought about Daniel's text, still unanswered on his phone. He thought about his mother, whom he hadn't called in weeks. He thought about Emily, long gone now, probably happy with someone who actually showed up. He thought about the man he'd planned to be and the man he'd become, and the distance between them felt like an ocean.

He put his head in his hands and closed his eyes.

"Mind if I sit?"

Adam's head jerked up.

A man was standing a few feet away, hands in his pockets, looking at Adam with an expression that was hard to read. He was dressed simply—khakis, a button-down shirt, no tie. He looked familiar, but it took Adam a moment to place him.

Then it clicked.

"Joshua?"

Joshua smiled. It was the same smile Adam remembered from years ago—warm, unhurried, like he had all the time in the world.

"Hello, Adam."

Adam stared at him, too stunned to speak. Joshua walked over and sat down on the pallets beside him, looking out at the alley behind the building as if this were the most natural thing in the world.

"What are you—" Adam shook his head, trying to clear it. "How did you—why are you here?"

"I was in the area," Joshua said. "Thought I'd stop by."

"The loading dock?"

Joshua shrugged. "Seemed like the right place to look."

It didn't make sense. None of it made sense. But Adam was too tired to argue, too empty to question. He just sat there, side by side with a man he hadn't seen in years, watching a pigeon peck at crumbs on the concrete.

They sat in silence for a while. It should have been awkward, but somehow it wasn't. Joshua didn't seem to need Adam to say anything. He just sat there, present, patient, as if waiting was something he was very good at.

Finally, Joshua spoke.

"Is this the life you wanted?"

The question hit Adam like a physical blow.

He thought about his corner office, his title, his salary. He thought about the panic attacks and the whiskey and the pills.

CHAPTER TEN

He thought about the lies he'd told, the friendships he'd abandoned, and the man he'd destroyed to protect himself.

He thought about the boy who'd sat in an empty apartment two years ago, holding two letters, dreaming of greatness.

"No," he said. His voice cracked. "No, this isn't—I didn't want—"

He couldn't finish. The words jammed in his throat, and then, to his horror, he was crying. Not quiet, dignified tears—ugly, heaving sobs that shook his whole body. Years of grief and shame and loneliness poured out of him, and he couldn't stop it, couldn't control it, couldn't do anything but break.

Joshua didn't say anything. He just put a hand on Adam's shoulder and let him weep.

When Adam finally ran out of tears, he wiped his face with his sleeve, embarrassed, exhausted, and emptied out.

"I'm sorry," he muttered. "I don't know what—"

"Don't apologize." Joshua's voice was gentle. "You needed that."

Adam laughed bitterly. "What I need is a time machine. Go back two years, and make a different choice. But it's too late for that now."

"Is it?"

Adam turned to look at him. Joshua's eyes were kind, but there was something else in them—something steady and certain, like a man who knew things other people didn't.

"You can't undo the past," Joshua said. "No one can. But you can choose what happens next. You can walk out of here, Adam. Today. Right now."

"You don't understand." Adam shook his head. "The non-compete, the clawbacks—I'm trapped. I owe them money. If I leave, Lucian will destroy me. He'll make calls and ruin my reputation—I've seen him do it. I can't just walk away."

"What if you didn't have to worry about any of that?"

Adam frowned. "What do you mean?"

Joshua leaned forward, his elbows on his knees, his gaze fixed on Adam's.

"The offer is still open, Adam. It never closed. There's a place for you at Light Co.—a real place, not a position to be filled, but a seat at the table. And the cost of leaving here, the debt, the legal threats, the reputation—" He paused. "My Father can cover all of it."

Adam stared at him. "That's... that's not possible. You don't know how much—"

"I know exactly how much." Joshua's voice was quiet but certain. "Every dollar. Every clause. Every threat Lucian could make. And I'm telling you—it's covered. All of it. You just have to choose to walk out the door."

Adam's mind was spinning. It didn't make sense. Companies didn't do this. People didn't do this. You didn't rescue someone who'd rejected you, who'd chosen your competitor, who'd spent two years becoming everything they'd promised they wouldn't be.

"Why?" he asked. "Why would you do this? I turned you down. I chose *them*. I've done things—terrible things—"

"I know."

"Then why?"

Joshua smiled—a smile full of something Adam couldn't name. Sorrow and joy, woven together. Love that hurt because it saw everything and chose to love anyway.

"Because that's who my Father is," he said. "And that's who I am. We don't give up on people, Adam. We come and find them."

Adam sat in silence, letting the words sink in.

He didn't understand it. He couldn't understand it. Grace this big didn't fit in his categories, didn't match anything he'd learned in business school or in the glass tower of Fyre Inc.

But he wanted it. God help him, he wanted it.

"I don't know if I can do it," he said quietly. "Walk away. Face Lucian. Face what I've become."

"You don't have to do it alone." Joshua stood up, brushing off his pants, and extended his hand. "When you're ready to leave, I'll be there. I'll walk out with you."

CHAPTER TEN

Adam looked at the hand. It was an ordinary hand—calloused, like someone who worked with them. But the offer it represented was anything but ordinary.

"How do I reach you?" Adam asked.

Joshua smiled. "Just call. I'll hear you."

He turned and walked across the loading dock, disappearing around the corner of the building. Adam watched him go, heart pounding, mind racing.

For the first time in two years, something stirred in his chest that felt almost like hope.

He didn't deserve it. He knew that.

But maybe that was the point.

Chapter Eleven

THE COST

Adam didn't sleep that night.

He lay in bed, staring at the ceiling, replaying the conversation on the loading dock. Joshua's words circled in his mind like birds that wouldn't land: *The offer is still open. My Father can cover all of it.*

It was too good to be true. That was the problem. Adam had spent enough years in business to know that nothing came free. Every gift had strings. Every favor created a debt. The world ran on transactions, and anyone who pretended otherwise was either naïve or lying.

And yet.

There had been something in Joshua's eyes that didn't fit the categories Adam knew. Something that looked like it might actually be what it claimed to be.

At three in the morning, he gave up on sleep. He made coffee, pulled out his contract, and spread it across the kitchen table one more time. He needed to understand exactly what he was dealing with. He needed to know the size of the cage before he could believe anyone could open it.

The numbers were worse than he remembered.

The signing bonus clawback: $85,000. The relocation

package repayment: $40,000. The unvested stock options he'd forfeit: worth nearly $200,000 at current valuation. The non-compete clause that would bar him from working in his field for two years. The reputation damage Lucian could inflict with a few well-placed phone calls.

Adam added it up, subtracted his savings, and stared at the result. Even if he liquidated everything he owned, he'd still be over a hundred thousand dollars short. And that didn't account for the two years of unemployment the non-compete would create, or the black mark on his record, or the whisper campaign Lucian would wage.

He put his head in his hands.

My Father can cover all of it, Joshua had said.

Impossible. It had to be impossible.

He called Joshua the next morning.

He didn't have a number—Joshua hadn't given him one—but he found Light Co.'s main line on the internet and asked to be transferred. The receptionist didn't hesitate, didn't ask for a reason, just said, "One moment, please," and the next voice Adam heard was Joshua's.

"Adam." He sounded pleased but not surprised. "I was hoping you'd call."

"I need to understand," Adam said. His voice was hoarse from the sleepless night. "What you said yesterday—about covering the cost. I need to understand what that means."

"Can you meet me?" Joshua asked. "There's a coffee shop on Maple Street, near the park. I can be there in an hour."

Adam said yes. He didn't know what else to say.

The coffee shop was small and quiet, the kind of place with mismatched furniture and local art on the walls. Joshua was already there when Adam arrived, sitting at a table near the window with two cups of coffee.

"I took a guess on your order," Joshua said, sliding one across the table. "Black, two sugars."

Adam stared at him. It was exactly how he took his coffee.

CHAPTER ELEVEN

He hadn't told Joshua that.

He sat down, wrapping his hands around the warm cup, trying to find the words. "I ran the numbers last night," he finally said. "The clawbacks, the non-compete, everything. I owe Fyre Inc. over $125,000 if I leave. And that's before Lucian starts making calls."

Joshua nodded. "I know."

"You know?"

"I know everything, Adam. The exact amount. The terms. The way Lucian operates." Joshua's voice was calm, matter-of-fact. "I know what it will cost for you to walk away. And I'm telling you—it's covered."

"How?" Adam's voice cracked. "How is that possible? No company just—writes a check for someone else's debts. No one pays that kind of price for a stranger."

"You're not a stranger."

"I rejected your offer. I chose your competitor. I've spent two years becoming—" Adam stopped, his throat tight. "I'm not worth this. You have to know that. I'm not worth what it would cost."

Joshua was quiet for a moment. Then he leaned forward, his eyes holding Adam's.

"Let me tell you how this works," he said. "You're right—there's a cost. A real cost. The debt has to be paid. The contracts have to be satisfied. Someone has to absorb the penalty for breaking them."

"So what—I'd owe Light Co. instead? I'd be trading one debt for another?"

"No." Joshua shook his head. "You wouldn't owe us anything. The cost isn't transferred to you, Adam. It's absorbed. By me."

Adam frowned. "I don't understand."

"When you walk out of Fyre Inc., Lucian will come after you. He'll demand the money. He'll threaten legal action. He'll try to destroy your reputation." Joshua's voice was steady, his eyes never leaving Adam's. "But he won't find you. He'll find me. I'll pay the debt. I'll face the lawyers. I'll take whatever Lucian throws at you. That's my job. That's what I do."

"Why?" It came out as a whisper.

Joshua smiled—that same sad, joyful smile from the loading dock.

"Because my Father loves you. Because I love you. Because that's what love does—it pays the price the other person can't pay." He paused. "You don't have to earn it, Adam. You can't earn it. It's a gift. All you have to do is accept it."

Adam sat in silence, his coffee growing cold in his hands.

Everything in him rebelled against it. His whole life, he'd been taught that you got what you earned. You worked hard, you climbed the ladder, you paid your dues. Nothing was free. Nothing was given. You made your own way or you didn't make it at all.

But that philosophy had brought him here—to a golden cage, a hollow life, a soul so compromised he barely recognized himself. The gospel of self-reliance had made him successful and miserable, powerful and empty, and rich in everything except what mattered.

And here was Joshua, offering something completely different. Not a transaction, but a gift. Not an exchange, but a rescue.

"What if I fail?" Adam asked quietly. "What if I come to Light Co. and I'm not good enough? What if I mess up again?"

"You will," Joshua said simply. "You'll fail. You'll mess up. You'll fall short. That's not the question."

"Then what is?"

"The question is whether you'll let us love you anyway." Joshua reached across the table and put his hand over Adam's. "At Fyre Inc., your value depends on your performance. If you produce, you're valuable. If you don't, you're disposable. That's not how we work. At Light Co., you're valuable because you're *you*. Not because of what you do. Because of who you are."

CHAPTER ELEVEN

Adam felt something shift inside him—something old and heavy beginning to break loose.

"I want to believe that," he said. "I want to believe it's real."

"Then take the first step." Joshua squeezed his hand, then let go. "You don't have to have it all figured out. You don't have to feel ready. You just have to choose to walk out the door." He paused. "And when you do, I'll be there. Just like I promised."

Adam looked at him—this strange, quiet man who had appeared on a loading dock and offered to pay a debt he hadn't incurred for a person who didn't deserve it.

It didn't make sense. It would never make sense.

But maybe that was what grace was—something too big for sense, too generous for logic, and too good for a world that ran on transactions and debts.

"Okay," Adam said. His voice was barely above a whisper. "Okay. I'll do it. I'll walk out."

Joshua's face broke into a smile—a real smile, full and unguarded, like the sun coming out from behind clouds.

"When?"

Adam took a deep breath. His heart was pounding, his hands were shaking, and for the first time in two years, he felt completely, terrifyingly alive.

"Tomorrow," he said. "Tomorrow morning."

Chapter Twelve

THE ESCAPE

Adam arrived at Fyre Inc. at 8:00 a.m., one hour before his meeting with Lucian.

He'd barely slept, but for once it wasn't anxiety keeping him awake. It was something else—a strange, humming energy that felt almost like anticipation. Like standing at the edge of a cliff, about to jump, knowing the fall would either kill you or teach you to fly.

He took the elevator to the thirty-eighth floor and walked to his corner office one last time. Everything looked the same—the sleek desk, the leather chair, the view of the river that had once made him feel like a king. He'd spent two years here, and now it felt like looking at someone else's life.

He didn't pack anything. There was nothing here he wanted to keep.

At 8:45, he printed a single page—his resignation letter, three sentences long—and walked to Lucian's office.

The CEO's assistant waved him in without a word. Lucian was behind his desk, silhouetted against the floor-to-ceiling windows, the city sprawling beneath him like a conquered kingdom. He looked up as Adam entered, and his smile was warm, welcoming—the smile of a man who had no idea what was coming.

"Adam. Good to see you. Have a seat."

Adam didn't sit.

"I'm resigning," he said. "Effective immediately."

He placed the letter on Lucian's desk.

For a moment, nothing happened. Lucian stared at the paper as if it were written in a language he didn't recognize. Then, slowly, his smile faded. His eyes lifted to meet Adam's, and the warmth drained out of them like water from a sink.

"I'm sorry?"

"I'm leaving, Lucian. Today. I'm done."

Lucian leaned back in his chair. He picked up the letter, glanced at it, set it down. When he spoke again, his voice was still calm, but there was something underneath it now—something cold, something coiled.

"I see." He steepled his fingers. "And where exactly do you think you're going?"

"Light Co."

Something flickered in Lucian's eyes. Recognition. And something else—was it hatred? Fear? Adam couldn't tell.

"Light Co.," Lucian repeated. "Interesting choice." He stood up and walked around the desk, moving slowly, deliberately, until he was standing directly in front of Adam. "Do you have any idea what you're giving up? The stock options alone—"

"I know what I'm giving up."

"Do you?" Lucian's voice dropped. "The non-compete clause in your contract prohibits you from working for any competitor for two years. Light Co. qualifies. If you walk out that door, I will enforce it. Every clause, every penalty, every dollar you owe us."

"I understand."

"I will destroy your reputation." Lucian's voice was soft now, almost gentle, but his eyes were ice. "Every contact you have in this industry—every door, every opportunity—I will close it. You will never work in this field again. Is that what you want?"

CHAPTER TWELVE

Adam's heart was pounding. His palms were sweating. Every instinct screamed at him to back down, apologize, and say it was a mistake. This was Lucian Fyre. This was the man who had made careers and ended them, who held the futures of hundreds of people in his manicured hands.

But he thought of Joshua. *I'll be there. I'll walk out with you.*

"Yes," Adam said. "This is what I want."

Lucian studied him for a long moment. The mask of charm was gone now, and what lay beneath it was something ancient and cold—a darkness that had always been there, hidden behind the smile, the flattery, and the talk of family.

"You disappoint me, Adam." His voice was flat. "I saw such potential in you. I gave you everything—the office, the title, the future. And this is how you repay me?"

"You gave me a cage," Adam said quietly. "A beautiful cage with golden bars. But it was still a cage."

Lucian's jaw tightened. "You think Light Co. is any different? You think their *Father*"—he said the word like a curse—"will give you anything better? It's all the same game, Adam. The only difference is who's holding the leash."

"No." Adam shook his head. "It's not."

He turned and walked toward the door.

"You'll regret this." Lucian's voice followed him, sharp and venomous. "You'll come crawling back, and when you do, I won't be so generous. I'll make sure you have nothing—no job, no reputation, no future. You'll be *nothing*."

Adam paused at the door. He didn't turn around.

"I was already nothing," he said. "I just didn't know it."

And he walked out.

The elevator ride down was the longest of Adam's life.

He watched the numbers descend—40, 39, 38—and felt his old life peeling away with each floor. The corner office. The title. The salary. The future he'd sold his soul to build. All of it, gone. He had nothing now except a promise from a man he barely knew.

The doors opened onto the lobby.

Joshua was standing by the fountain.

He looked exactly as he had on the loading dock—calm, unhurried, like a man who had been waiting patiently and would wait as long as it took. When he saw Adam, he smiled.

"Ready?"

Adam nodded. He didn't trust his voice.

They walked out together—through the marble lobby, past the receptionist who watched with wide eyes, past the security desk, through the glass doors, and into the morning sunlight.

Adam stopped on the sidewalk and looked up at the tower. Forty stories of glass and steel, glittering in the sun. Somewhere up there, Lucian was watching. Adam could feel his gaze like a physical weight.

He didn't wave. He didn't gloat. He just turned and walked away.

Joshua fell into step beside him, and together they walked down the street, leaving the tower behind. The city hummed around them—traffic, pedestrians, the ordinary rhythm of a Tuesday morning. Adam had walked these blocks a thousand times, but they felt different now. Brighter. Freer.

"How do you feel?" Joshua asked.

Adam thought about it. He had just thrown away everything he'd spent two years building. He had made an enemy of one of the most powerful men in the industry. He had no job, no income, no plan beyond the next ten minutes.

And yet.

"Free," he said. "I feel free."

Joshua nodded, as if this were exactly the right answer.

"That's because you are," he said. "For the first time in two years, you're free."

They kept walking, away from the glass tower, toward something Adam couldn't see but was beginning, just barely, to believe in.

Behind them, the tower shrank against the sky until it was just another building among thousands.

Adam didn't look back.

Chapter Thirteen

THE FIRST MORNING

Adam woke up before his alarm.

He lay in bed for a moment, disoriented, waiting for the familiar weight to settle on his chest—the dread, the anxiety, the low hum of panic that had greeted him every morning for two years.

It didn't come.

He sat up slowly, as if moving too fast might summon it back. Sunlight was streaming through the window—real sunlight, not the gray glow of a city dawn. He'd moved out of the company apartment a week ago, into a small place outside the city, closer to Light Co. It had a yard. Birds sang in the mornings. He'd forgotten birds existed.

He showered, dressed, and made coffee. The motions were the same as always, but they felt different—lighter, somehow, as if gravity had loosened its grip. He caught himself humming while he poured his cereal and stopped, surprised. He couldn't remember the last time he'd hummed.

Today was his first day at Light Co.

The thought didn't fill him with anxiety. It filled him with something else—something fragile and unfamiliar that he was almost afraid to name.

Hope. It felt like hope.

The drive to Light Co. took twenty minutes through winding country roads. Adam rolled down his window and let the spring air wash over him—cool and clean, smelling of cut grass and something blooming. The trees were green, impossibly green, the kind of green he'd stopped noticing during his years in the glass tower.

He'd made this drive once before, two years ago, for his interview with Joshua. He'd been a different person then—ambitious, hungry, certain he knew what success looked like. He'd seen Light Co.'s brick buildings and green lawns and thought, *Ordinary*.

Now, pulling into the parking lot, he thought, *Home*.

The word surprised him. He'd never felt at home anywhere—not in the corner office, not in the luxury apartment, not even in the house where he'd grown up. Home had always been something to achieve, a destination at the end of the climb. He'd never imagined it could be a place you simply arrived at, welcomed before you'd proven anything.

He parked his car—the Honda he'd had since college, not the BMW Fyre Inc. had given him—and walked toward the entrance.

A woman was waiting for him in the lobby.

She was about his age, with dark hair pulled back in a ponytail and a warm, easy smile. She extended her hand as he approached.

"Adam? I'm Elena Torres. I'll be showing you around today."

Her handshake was firm and unhurried. She looked at him the way Joshua did—not evaluating, not measuring, just seeing.

"Welcome to Light Co.," she said. "We're glad you're here."

The words were simple, but something in her voice made Adam believe them. Not the polished welcome of Fyre Inc.'s orientation—not "you're the top one percent" or "you belong with us." Just: "We're glad you're here."

CHAPTER THIRTEEN

It was enough. More than enough.

Elena led him through the building, pointing out the workspaces, the break rooms, the small library tucked into a corner of the second floor. People smiled as they passed—real smiles, not the tight, performative ones Adam had grown used to. Someone waved. Someone else called out, "Hey, you must be Adam! Welcome aboard!"

Adam nodded and waved back, feeling strangely off-balance. At Fyre Inc., new hires were competitors. You watched them to see if they were a threat. Here, people seemed genuinely pleased to see him.

"It takes some getting used to," Elena said, as if reading his mind. "I came from a place like where you came from. The first few weeks, I kept waiting for the other shoe to drop."

Adam looked at her. "Did it?"

She smiled. "Still waiting. That was six years ago."

His desk was on the second floor, near a window that looked out over the gardens. It wasn't a corner office. It wasn't even a private office—just a desk in an open workspace, surrounded by other desks and other people.

It was perfect.

On the desk was a small card, handwritten: *Welcome, Adam. We're glad you're finally here.* —*The Father*

Adam picked it up and read it three times. *Finally here.* As if they'd been waiting for him. As if his arrival had always been expected, even when he'd been running in the other direction.

He set the card down carefully and got to work.

The work was different than he'd expected. Not easier—just different. There were no impossible deadlines, no moving targets, and no sense that failure meant destruction. Elena explained the project he'd be joining, answered his questions patiently, and told him to ask for help whenever he needed it.

"We don't do sink or swim here," she said. "That's not how people grow."

Adam thought of Claire, his old manager, telling him on

his first day at Fyre Inc.: *Sink or swim. That's how we find out what you're made of.*

Two different philosophies. Two different worlds.

At noon, someone rang a bell. Adam looked up, confused, and saw people standing, stretching, and heading toward the doors.

"Lunch," Elena said. "We eat together, usually outside when the weather's nice. Come on."

They walked outside to the gardens, where long tables had been set up in the sun. Food was spread out—simple, good food, the kind you actually wanted to eat. People sat together, laughing, talking, and sharing plates. No one was hunched over a laptop. No one was checking their phone with that anxious twitch Adam knew so well.

Adam filled a plate and found a spot at one of the tables. The sun was warm on his face. The food tasted like food—not the catered artisan meals of Fyre Inc., designed to impress, but real food, made by real people, meant to nourish.

He took a bite, and something broke open inside him.

It wasn't the food. It was everything—the sun, the garden, the sound of laughter, the absence of dread. For two years, he'd been dead. He knew that now. Walking and talking and succeeding, but dead. Numb to beauty, blind to joy, so focused on climbing that he'd forgotten what it felt like to simply be.

And now he was alive.

He didn't know how else to describe it. Something that had been asleep had woken up. Something that had been locked had been opened. He was *alive*, and he hadn't even known he'd been dead until now.

He set down his fork and looked up at the sky—bright blue, impossibly blue—and felt tears prick his eyes.

That afternoon, during a break, Adam stepped outside and called his mother.

She answered on the second ring, and her voice was wary, careful—the voice of a woman who'd learned not to expect too much from these calls.

CHAPTER THIRTEEN

"Adam? Is everything okay?"

"Yeah, Mom." His voice came out thick. "Everything's okay. Everything's..." He stopped and swallowed hard. "I'm at Light Co. It's my first day. And I just—I wanted to hear your voice."

Silence. Then: "Oh, honey."

And she was crying. He could hear it—soft, quiet tears, the kind she'd probably been holding back for two years.

"I'm sorry, Mom." The words came out broken. "I'm so sorry. For everything. For not calling. For not coming home. For becoming someone I—someone you didn't raise me to be."

"You're home now," she said. "That's all that matters. You're home now."

They talked for twenty minutes—about nothing, about everything. She told him about the garden, about his father's bad knee, and about the neighbors' new dog. He told her about the drive, about Elena, and about the sunlight in the garden. Neither of them said anything profound. They didn't have to.

When Adam hung up, he stood for a while in the garden, letting the sun warm his face. The world was the same as it had been yesterday, but he was different. Something had shifted. Something had healed.

He was alive.

For the first time in longer than he could remember, Adam Cole was truly, fully, miraculously alive.

Chapter Fourteen

MEETING THE FATHER

Three weeks into his new job, Adam was summoned to meet the Father.

The message came through Elena, delivered casually at the end of the day. "Oh, by the way—the Father would like to see you tomorrow morning. Nine o'clock, third floor, corner office."

Adam's stomach dropped.

He'd heard about the Father, of course. Everyone at Light Co. spoke of him with a kind of quiet reverence—not fear, exactly, but something deeper. Respect. Affection. The way people talk about someone who has shaped their lives in ways they're still discovering.

But Adam had never met him. He'd seen him once, at a distance—a tall figure walking through the gardens with Joshua, deep in conversation. He'd seemed ordinary from far away. Just a man. Just a CEO.

And yet.

Adam went home that night and couldn't sleep. His mind kept returning to the only frame of reference he had: Lucian Fyre. Corner office. CEO. Power. Those words meant something specific to him now—they meant danger, control, the constant evaluation of his worth. What if the Father was just a gentler version of the same thing? What if the kindness was just another mask?

He thought about all the mistakes he'd made at Fyre Inc. The lies. The compromises. Daniel. Did the Father know about all of that? Of course he did. Joshua knew. Which meant the Father knew.

Adam stared at the ceiling and wondered what he would say when confronted with the full weight of who he'd been.

The next morning, Adam climbed the stairs to the third floor with his heart pounding.

The corner office wasn't hard to find, but it wasn't what he expected. At Fyre Inc., Lucian's office had been a fortress—glass walls that turned opaque at the touch of a button, a door that was always closed, and an assistant who guarded access like a dragon guarding gold.

The Father's door was open.

Not ajar—fully open, propped wide, as if closing it had never occurred to anyone. Adam could see inside from the hallway: a simple desk, bookshelves, and windows that looked out over the gardens. No throne. No statement furniture. Just a room where someone worked.

He knocked on the doorframe, and a voice called out: "Come in, Adam."

Adam stepped inside.

The Father stood up from behind his desk—not to assert dominance, the way Lucian would have, but simply to greet him. He was older than Adam had expected, with gray hair and deep lines around his eyes, but there was something about him that defied age. A steadiness. A weight. The sense that he had seen everything and chosen, somehow, to remain kind.

"Adam." The Father extended his hand. His grip was warm and firm. "I've been looking forward to meeting you."

"Thank you, sir. I—"

"Please." The Father smiled and gestured to a chair across

CHAPTER FOURTEEN

from his desk. "Sit. And there's no need for 'sir.' Around here, most people just call me Father."

Adam sat, trying to steady his breathing. The Father settled into his own chair, not behind the desk but in another chair beside it, so they were sitting at the same level, facing each other like two people having a conversation rather than a boss evaluating an employee.

"How are you settling in?" the Father asked.

"Good. Really good." Adam hesitated. "Better than I deserve, honestly."

The Father tilted his head slightly. "Why do you say that?"

Adam looked down at his hands. He'd rehearsed this conversation a dozen times in his head, imagining how he'd defend himself, explain his choices, minimize his failures. But sitting here, in this quiet room with the door open and the sunlight streaming in, all of that fell away.

"Because of what I did," he said quietly. "At Fyre Inc. The things I compromised. The people I hurt." He swallowed. "There was a man—Daniel. I could have saved his job, and I didn't. I let him take the fall to protect myself. I've done things I'm not proud of. A lot of things."

He forced himself to look up, bracing for judgment. For disappointment. For the careful distance that would come when someone saw who you really were.

The Father was watching him with an expression Adam couldn't read. It wasn't shock—he clearly knew all of this already. It wasn't condemnation. It was something else. Something that looked almost like … tenderness.

"Adam," the Father said, "do you think I invited you here to review your failures?"

"I—" Adam stopped. He didn't know what to say.

"I know your story," the Father continued. "All of it. Joshua told me, years ago, when you first interviewed here. And I've been watching ever since—not to catch you failing, but because I cared about what would happen to you. When you chose Fyre Inc., it grieved me. When I saw what it was doing to you, it grieved me more."

He leaned forward, and his eyes held Adam's.

"But I didn't bring you here to talk about who you were. I brought you here to talk about who you're becoming."

Adam felt something break loose in his chest.

He had been prepared for many things. An interrogation. A probationary warning. The careful, conditional acceptance of a boss willing to overlook his past as long as he performed. That was how the world worked. That was how Fyre Inc. worked. Your value was what you produced, and your past was a debt you could never fully pay.

But this—this was something different.

"I don't understand," Adam said. "How can you just ... not care about what I did? How can you trust me after everything?"

The Father was quiet for a moment. Then he stood and walked to the window, looking out at the gardens below.

"I didn't say I don't care," he said. "What happened at Fyre Inc. mattered. It hurt you. It hurt others. That's real, and I won't pretend it isn't." He turned back to Adam. "But the cost of that has been paid. Joshua saw to it. Every debt, every penalty, every consequence—he absorbed it. You walked out of Fyre Inc. clean, Adam. Not because you earned it, but because he paid for it."

Adam thought of Joshua in the lobby, waiting for him. Joshua on the loading dock, sitting beside him in silence. Joshua at the coffee shop, saying, *I'll pay the debt. I'll take whatever Lucian throws at you.*

"So when I look at you," the Father continued, "I don't see a man defined by his failures. I see a man my son was willing to pay everything for. That's how much you matter. That's how much you've always mattered."

Adam's vision blurred. He blinked hard, trying to hold himself together.

CHAPTER FOURTEEN

"I don't know what to say," he managed.

The Father smiled—a warm, unhurried smile that reminded Adam, suddenly and powerfully, of Joshua.

"You don't have to say anything. You just have to receive it." He walked back to his chair and sat down. "Adam, you have a place here. A real place—not a position you have to earn, but a seat at the table because you belong. I'm not going to evaluate you, measure you, or discard you when you fall short. You're going to fall short. Everyone does. That's not what this is about."

"Then what is it about?"

The Father leaned back, and his eyes crinkled with something that looked like joy.

"It's about becoming who you were made to be. Discovering the work you were created for. Learning to live—really live—instead of just surviving." He paused. "You've spent years building someone else's kingdom, Adam. Now it's time to find out who you are when you're not striving, not performing, not trying to earn your worth. That's the journey ahead of you. And I'm going to be here for all of it."

Adam left the Father's office an hour later, dazed and quiet.

They had talked about other things—about Adam's work, his interests, and his family. The Father had asked about his parents, knew his mother's name, and knew that his father had worked the same job for thirty years. He asked questions not to extract information but because he genuinely wanted to know. And when Adam talked, the Father listened—really listened—in a way that made Adam feel like the most important person in the world.

Not because of what he could produce. Just because he was Adam.

He walked back to his desk in a kind of trance. Elena looked up as he passed and smiled knowingly.

"First meeting with the Father?"

Adam nodded, not trusting his voice.

"Yeah." She laughed softly. "It's a lot. I cried for an hour after mine."

Adam sat down at his desk and looked out the window at the gardens, the sunlight, the ordinary miraculous beauty of a Tuesday morning.

He thought about worth. About value. About all the years he'd spent trying to earn something that, it turned out, had been offered freely all along.

He didn't understand it. He wasn't sure he ever would.

But for the first time in his life, Adam Cole knew—not just believed, but knew—that he was loved. Not for what he did. Not for what he could become. But simply, impossibly, unconditionally, for who he already was.

It was, he realized, the only thing he'd ever really wanted.

And it had been waiting for him all along.

Chapter Fifteen

LEARNING TO WORK AGAIN

The old habits died hard.

Two months into his time at Light Co., Adam still arrived before everyone else and left after everyone else. He still checked his email compulsively, still felt a spike of panic whenever his phone buzzed, still measured his days by what he'd produced rather than who he'd become.

One evening, Elena found him at his desk at seven o'clock, the office empty around him, his eyes fixed on a spreadsheet he'd already reviewed three times.

"Adam." She stood in the doorway, her bag over her shoulder, her coat already on. "What are you still doing here?"

"Just finishing up." He didn't look away from the screen. "I want to make sure this analysis is perfect before the meeting tomorrow."

Elena walked over and sat on the edge of his desk, blocking his view. "The analysis was good three hours ago. I reviewed it myself."

"I know, but—"

"But what?" Her voice was gentle but direct. "What happens if it's not perfect? What happens if you miss something?"

Adam opened his mouth to answer, then stopped. At Fyre Inc., the answer had been clear: failure meant exposure.

Weakness meant vulnerability. One mistake could unravel everything. But here...

"I don't know," he admitted.

Elena smiled. "Nothing. That's the answer. If you miss something, we catch it together. If it's not perfect, we fix it. No one's going to fire you. No one's going to think less of you." She paused. "You're not earning your place here, Adam. You already have it."

She stood up and nodded toward the door. "Go home. Rest. The work will be here tomorrow."

Adam looked at the spreadsheet one more time. Then he closed his laptop and left.

The unlearning happened slowly, in small moments he almost didn't notice.

The first time he admitted he didn't know something in a meeting, bracing for the flicker of contempt that always followed at Fyre Inc.—and instead, someone simply said, "No problem, let me show you."

The first time he pushed back on a deadline, explaining that the work needed more time to be done well—and instead of being labeled difficult, he was thanked for his honesty.

The first time he made a real mistake—a calculation error that delayed a project by a week—and waited for the hammer to fall. Joshua stopped by his desk that afternoon, not to reprimand him, but to ask how he was doing.

"Mistakes happen," Joshua said, leaning against the cubicle wall. "They're not the end of the world. They're how we learn."

"At Fyre Inc.—" Adam started.

"You're not at Fyre Inc. anymore." Joshua's voice was kind but firm. "You don't have to live by their rules. You never did, really. You just thought you did."

Adam sat with that for a long time after Joshua left. *You never did, really. You just thought you did.*

How many of the chains he'd worn had been real, and how many had been illusions he'd believed into existence?

CHAPTER FIFTEEN

As the months passed, Adam began to discover parts of himself he'd buried.

He'd always been good with numbers—that was what Fyre Inc. had valued, what they'd used. But here, he found he was good at other things too. He had a knack for explaining complex ideas simply. He was patient with new team members in a way his managers at Fyre Inc. had never been patient with him. He noticed when people were struggling and found himself offering help without being asked.

One afternoon, a young analyst named Micah came to him with a problem—a model that wouldn't balance, numbers that didn't make sense. Adam could have fixed it himself in ten minutes. Instead, he sat with Micah for an hour, walking through the logic, asking questions, letting the young man find the error himself.

When Micah finally spotted the mistake, his face lit up. "Thank you," he said. "No one's ever taken the time to actually teach me before."

Adam thought of himself at Fyre Inc., drowning and afraid to ask for help. He thought of Claire saying, *Sink or swim*. He thought of all the hours he'd spent terrified of being exposed as inadequate.

"Anytime," he told Micah. And meant it.

The work itself was different too.

At Fyre Inc., Adam had worked on projects designed to maximize profit, regardless of who they helped or hurt. The clients were abstractions—names on spreadsheets, sources of revenue. The goal was always the same: more. More growth, more market share, more zeros on the bottom line.

At Light Co., the work had a different purpose. The clients were real people—small businesses trying to survive, nonprofits trying to serve their communities, families trying to build something that would last. Adam found himself caring about outcomes in a way he never had before. Not because his bonus depended on it, but because the work actually *mattered*.

One project stood out. A small nonprofit that ran an after-school program was on the verge of closing—their finances were a mess, their systems were outdated, and they didn't have the resources to fix any of it. Light Co. took them on pro bono, and Adam was assigned to lead the engagement.

He spent three months with them, untangling their books, setting up new systems, training their staff. It wasn't glamorous work. There was no corner office waiting at the end, no bonus, no recognition beyond a handwritten thank-you card from the director.

But on the last day, when he visited the center and saw the kids streaming in after school—laughing, doing homework, eating snacks—he felt something he'd never felt at Fyre Inc.

Pride. Real pride. Not the hollow satisfaction of a closed deal, but the deep, quiet joy of having done something good.

This was what work was supposed to be, he realized. Not a transaction—time for money, labor for worth. But an offering. A way of putting something into the world that hadn't been there before.

But there was one thing Adam still hadn't done. One debt that grace had paid but honesty still required.

Daniel Chen.

The name had haunted him since the day he'd walked out of Fyre Inc. He'd never answered Daniel's text—the one where Daniel had apologized to *him*, worried about *Adam's* reputation, even as his own career lay in ruins. The memory of that message was a splinter in Adam's conscience that wouldn't work itself out.

He brought it up with Joshua one afternoon, during one of their walks through the gardens.

"There's someone I wronged," Adam said. "Before I came here. I let him take the blame for something that was partly my fault. He lost his job. And I never—I never made it right."

Joshua was quiet for a moment, his hands clasped behind his back. "What's stopping you?"

CHAPTER FIFTEEN

"Fear, I guess. Shame." Adam shook his head. "What do you even say to someone you've hurt that badly? 'Sorry' doesn't seem like enough."

"It's not," Joshua agreed. "But it's a start. And sometimes, grace doesn't just flow to us. It flows *through* us. To the people we've hurt. To the people still trapped where we used to be."

Adam thought about that. *The people still trapped where we used to be.*

"Do you know where he is now?" Joshua asked.

"No. After he was fired, he kind of disappeared. I heard he had trouble finding work—Lucian made sure of that." The old guilt twisted in Adam's stomach. "The last I heard, he was doing temp work somewhere. Contract stuff. Nothing like what he's capable of."

Joshua stopped walking and turned to face him. "Find him, Adam. Tell him the truth. And then—if he's willing—tell him about this place."

"You mean—"

"The offer is always open." Joshua smiled. "You know that better than anyone."

It took Adam two weeks to track Daniel down. Two weeks of searching LinkedIn, making calls, and following leads that went nowhere. Daniel had scrubbed most of his online presence—the digital equivalent of someone trying to disappear.

Finally, through a mutual acquaintance, Adam got a phone number. He sat in his car in the Light Co. parking lot for twenty minutes before he worked up the courage to dial.

Daniel answered on the fourth ring. "Hello?"

"Daniel. It's—it's Adam. Adam Cole."

Silence. A long, painful silence.

"Adam." Daniel's voice was flat, guarded. "I wasn't expecting to hear from you."

"I know. I should have called a long time ago." Adam gripped the steering wheel with his free hand. "Daniel, I need to tell you something. Can we meet? In person? There's—

there's something I need to say, and I don't want to do it over the phone."

Another silence. Adam could almost hear Daniel weighing it—the old loyalty against the old wound.

"Alright," Daniel said finally. "There's a coffee shop on Miller Street. Tomorrow, noon."

"I'll be there."

Daniel looked older than Adam remembered. Tired. The eager, earnest young man from Fyre Inc. had been replaced by someone warier, someone who had learned the hard way that the world wasn't kind to people who trusted too easily.

They sat across from each other at a small table by the window, cups of coffee cooling between them. Adam had rehearsed this conversation a hundred times, but now that he was here, the words felt impossibly inadequate.

"Daniel," he began, "I didn't come here to make excuses. I came to tell you the truth." He took a breath. "The error in the Hendricks model—I found it. Three weeks before the presentation. I fixed part of it, but I missed a linked file, and I never told anyone. When Lucian asked who was responsible, I could have spoken up. I could have told him what really happened. But I didn't."

Daniel's face didn't change, but something flickered in his eyes.

"I let you take the fall," Adam continued. "I was scared, and I was selfish, and I sacrificed you to protect myself. You lost your job because of me. You've struggled to find work because of what Lucian did to your reputation, and that happened because I was too much of a coward to tell the truth."

He looked Daniel in the eye. "I'm sorry. I know that doesn't fix anything. I know it doesn't give you back the last two years. But I needed you to know the truth. And I needed you to hear it from me."

Daniel was quiet for a long moment. He stared at his coffee, his jaw tight. When he finally spoke, his voice was rough.

CHAPTER FIFTEEN

"I wondered," he said. "For a long time, I wondered if there was something I didn't know. The timing never quite made sense. But I trusted you, Adam. I looked up to you."

"I know." The words were barely a whisper. "I know you did."

Daniel looked up at him. "Why now? Why tell me now, after all this time?"

Adam thought about how to answer. "Because I'm not at Fyre Inc. anymore. I left—or rather, I was rescued. There's another company, Light Co., run by a man named Joshua. He found me when I was at rock bottom, and he offered me a way out. Paid my debts, gave me a fresh start, and showed me a different way to live."

He leaned forward. "It changed everything, Daniel. I'm not the same person I was. And part of becoming someone new means facing the wrongs I did as the old one. I couldn't move forward without telling you the truth."

Daniel studied him for a long moment, as if weighing whether to believe him. Finally, something in his expression softened—not forgiveness, not yet, but the beginning of something. An opening.

"This place," Daniel said slowly. "Light Co. What's it like?"

Adam felt something lift in his chest. "It's different. Really different. The work matters. The people matter. And they don't—" He paused, searching for the right words. "They don't measure your worth by what you produce. They don't throw you away when you make a mistake. It's like…"

"Like what?"

"Like being part of a family. A real one."

Daniel was quiet again. Adam could see the hunger in his eyes—the longing for something he'd stopped believing existed.

"Daniel." Adam reached into his jacket and pulled out a card—simple, cream-colored, with the Light Co. logo embossed on the front. "There's a position open. Entry-level, but with room to grow. And the offer—" He smiled, hearing

Joshua's voice in his head. "The offer is always open. For as long as you need to think about it."

Daniel took the card. He turned it over in his hands, running his thumb across the logo.

"Why?" he asked quietly. "After what you did—why would you try to help me?"

Adam thought about Joshua on the loading dock. Joshua in the lobby. Joshua walking beside him out of Fyre Inc. and into the sunlight.

"Because someone helped me," he said. "When I didn't deserve it. When I'd made a mess of everything. Someone came and found me anyway." He paused. "I think that's how it's supposed to work. You receive grace, and then you pass it on. Not because you have to, but because once you've tasted it, you can't keep it to yourself."

Daniel looked at him for a long moment. Then, slowly, he nodded.

"I'll think about it," he said. And for the first time since Adam had sat down, something that looked almost like hope flickered in his eyes.

Daniel started at Light Co. three weeks later.

Adam was there on his first day—not as a manager or a mentor, but as a friend. He walked Daniel through the lobby, showed him the gardens, introduced him to Elena and the team. He watched Daniel's eyes widen at the same things Adam's had: the open doors, the unhurried pace, the people who smiled like they meant it.

And when Daniel sat down at his new desk, Adam placed a card there—handwritten, the same words Joshua had written for him:

Welcome, Daniel. We're glad you're finally here.

Daniel read it, and his eyes glistened.

"Thank you," he said quietly. "For coming to find me."

Adam smiled. "That's what we do here," he said. "We don't give up on people. We go and find them."

CHAPTER FIFTEEN

It was Joshua's line, borrowed and passed on. And Adam understood, finally, that this was what he'd been saved *for*—not just to escape Fyre Inc., not just to find healing for himself, but to go back for others. To be the Joshua for someone else that Joshua had been for him.

Grace wasn't meant to end with him. It was meant to flow through him, out into the world, carrying the offer that never expired to everyone still trapped in towers of glass and gold.

The offer is always open.

His job now was to make sure people knew.

Chapter Sixteen

THE LONG FAITHFULNESS

The years passed the way years do—slowly when you're living them, quickly when you look back.

Adam would remember his time at Light Co. not as a single story but as a series of moments, strung together like beads on a string. Some were small. Some were everything. All of them, he came to understand, were gifts.

He married Elena on a Saturday in October, three years after his first day at Light Co.

The wedding was small—family, friends, and colleagues who had become like family. They held it in the gardens at Light Co., with the Father's blessing, under a canopy of autumn leaves. Joshua performed the ceremony, which wasn't traditional but felt exactly right.

Adam's mother cried through the whole thing. His father stood beside her, quiet and proud, wearing the expensive watch Adam had sent him years ago—the apology gift, the inadequate substitute for presence. But things were different now. Adam had come home, really come home, and the distance between them had slowly, painfully, beautifully closed.

When Adam said his vows, his voice broke on the words *for better or for worse*. He knew what worse looked like now.

He'd lived it. And he knew, standing there with Elena's hands in his, that he would never walk that road alone again.

Their first child was born two years later. A daughter. They named her Grace.

Adam held her in the hospital, this tiny, impossibly fragile thing, and felt something shift in his chest—a love so fierce and immediate, it frightened him. He thought about his own father, holding him like this thirty years ago. He thought about all the birthdays he'd missed, all the phone calls he'd cut short, all the ways he'd chosen ambition over presence.

He made a promise, silent and fierce: *I will be there. I will show up. I will choose you. Every time.*

A son followed three years later. They named him David, after Adam's father.

When Adam told his father the name, the old man didn't say anything for a long moment. Then he turned away, and Adam saw his shoulders shake.

Some things don't need words. Some things are too big for them.

Adam's father died on a Tuesday morning in March, fifteen years after Adam had joined Light Co. It wasn't sudden. There had been months of decline—the cancer eating away at him slowly, giving them time to say what needed to be said. Adam drove home every weekend, sometimes more. He sat by his father's bed and talked about nothing—about baseball, about the kids, about the weather. His father listened, sometimes spoke, but mostly just held his hand.

Near the end, when words were hard, his father looked at him with those tired, loving eyes and said, "I'm proud of you, son. The man you've become."

Adam thought about all the years he'd spent trying to make his father proud through achievements—the degrees, the titles, the salary. None of it had mattered. What mattered was this: being there. Showing up. Choosing presence over performance.

CHAPTER SIXTEEN

"I love you, Dad," Adam said. "I'm sorry it took me so long to come home."

His father squeezed his hand. "You came. That's what matters. You came."

He died the next morning, with Adam and his mother beside him. Peaceful. Ready. The watch Adam had given him was still on his wrist.

There were hard seasons. Of course there were.

A year when Light Co. faced financial trouble, and everyone took pay cuts, and Adam wondered if he'd made a mistake leaving the security of Fyre Inc. A season when his marriage hit rocky ground, and he and Elena had to learn to fight fairly and forgive freely. A stretch of months when Grace struggled in school and nothing Adam did seemed to help.

But the difference—the difference that changed everything—was that he didn't face any of it alone.

When Light Co. struggled, the Father gathered everyone together and spoke honestly about the challenges, and they weathered it as a community. When his marriage strained, Joshua met with them, listened without judgment, and helped them find their way back to each other. When Grace struggled, Elena reminded him that children aren't problems to be solved but people to be loved.

The hard seasons passed. They always did. And on the other side, there was always more grace waiting. Not because Adam had earned it, but because that was how grace worked—inexhaustible, undeserved, and always more where that came from.

Over the years, Adam rose at Light Co.—not through striving, but through faithfulness.

He became a team lead, then a director, then a vice president. The titles came, but they meant something different here. Not power to be wielded, but responsibility to be stewarded. Not status to be protected, but opportunity to serve.

He mentored dozens of young employees over the years. Some came from places like Fyre Inc., broken and wary, waiting for the other shoe to drop. Adam recognized them immediately. He had been them.

He would sit with them in his office—door always open, the way the Father's was—and say the words he'd needed to hear: "You're not earning your place here. You already have it. The question isn't whether you'll fail—you will. The question is whether you'll let us love you anyway."

Joshua's words, passed on. The Father's grace, multiplied.

That was how it worked, Adam came to understand. Grace wasn't meant to be hoarded. It was meant to be given away—and somehow, in the giving, it grew.

Sometimes, late at night, Adam thought about Marcus Webb.

He'd tried to reach out after leaving Fyre Inc., but Marcus never responded. Years later, Adam heard through the grapevine that Marcus had finally left—not by choice, but pushed out in a corporate restructuring, replaced by someone younger and cheaper. Twenty years of loyalty, and Lucian had discarded him like a used tissue.

Adam tried to find him, to offer help, but Marcus had disappeared. Moved away. Started over. Or maybe just vanished, the way people do when the thing they'd built their identity on crumbles beneath them.

Adam prayed for him sometimes. It was the only thing he could do. He prayed that somewhere, somehow, Marcus had found his own loading dock. That he'd found Joshua. Found his way home.

The decades accumulated like compound interest—small deposits of faithfulness growing into something larger than Adam could have imagined.

He watched his children grow. Grace became a teacher—patient and kind, the way her mother was. David went into medicine, driven by a quiet desire to heal. They both knew the story of their father's journey, told in pieces over the years, and they carried it with them like a map for their own lives.

CHAPTER SIXTEEN

He watched his marriage deepen. The early passion softened into something steadier—a partnership, a friendship, a love that had been tested and proven true. Elena's hair went gray, and laugh lines gathered around her eyes, and Adam thought she had never been more beautiful.

He watched Light Co. thrive, not in the explosive way Fyre Inc. had pursued—endless growth, market domination—but in a quieter way. Sustainable. Healthy. A company that measured success not just in profit but in impact, in the lives touched and communities served.

And through it all, like a golden thread woven through the tapestry of his days, there was the Father's kindness. Showing up in expected places and unexpected ones. Deepening year by year. Never exhausted, never withdrawn, always more.

"The surpassing riches of his grace in kindness toward us," the Scripture said.

Adam hadn't understood those words when he was young. Now, forty years into his journey, he was beginning to.

Grace wasn't a single gift. It was a lifetime of gifts, one after another, each one revealing new depths of a love too vast to comprehend.

And the best part—the part that still amazed him, even after all these years—was that it wasn't over yet.

There was still more to come.

Chapter Seventeen

THE LAST WORKDAY

Adam Cole was sixty-five years old, and today was his last day of work.

He arrived early, the way he always had—not out of anxiety anymore, but out of habit, and because he wanted a few quiet moments before the day began. The parking lot was nearly empty, the morning mist still clinging to the gardens, the old brick building golden in the early light.

He sat in his car for a while, hands on the steering wheel, looking at the place that had been his home for forty years.

Forty years. It seemed impossible. He could still remember his first morning—the uncertainty, the hope, the tentative belief that maybe, just maybe, this place was different. He remembered Elena greeting him in the lobby. He remembered the Father's card on his desk: *We're glad you're finally here.*

Finally here. He was finally here. And now, somehow, it was time to leave.

He walked the halls slowly, taking his time, letting the memories rise.

The lobby, where Joshua had stood waiting for him the day he escaped Fyre Inc. The staircase he'd climbed with his heart pounding, on his way to meet the Father for the first time. The second-floor workspace where he'd sat at his desk and looked out at the gardens and felt, for the first time in years, truly alive.

His office now was on the third floor, near the Father's—a corner office, though he'd never asked for it. The door was always open, just like the Father's had always been. On the wall hung a single framed quote, the same one he'd noticed in the lobby on his first day: *We are his workmanship.*

He understood those words now. He had lived them.

Adam sat at his desk one last time. The surface was neat—he'd never been one for clutter—but personal touches had accumulated over the years. A photo of Elena on their wedding day. A crayon drawing Grace had made when she was five, now faded and precious. A baseball signed by David's Little League team, the year Adam had coached. A smooth stone from the garden, picked up during a walk with Joshua decades ago, kept for no reason except that it reminded him of that conversation.

He opened the top drawer. Inside was a card—yellowed now, the ink faded—that he'd kept for forty years. *Welcome, Adam. We're glad you're finally here. —The Father*

He held it for a moment, running his thumb over the handwriting. Then he tucked it into his jacket pocket, close to his heart.

By mid-morning, the office was full, and word had spread. People stopped by all day—colleagues, mentees, and friends. Some he'd worked with for decades. Some were young enough to be his grandchildren, new hires who knew him only as the gray-haired vice president with the open door and the listening ear.

They brought cards, small gifts, and memories. A woman named Sarah, whom he'd mentored fifteen years ago when she arrived broken from a toxic workplace, told him through tears that he'd changed her life. "You told me I wasn't earning my place," she said. "That I already had it. I've never forgotten that."

A young man named James, fresh out of college, shook his

CHAPTER SEVENTEEN

hand and said, "I hope I can be like you someday. The way you treat people—it's different. It matters."

Adam didn't know what to say to any of them. He had never thought of himself as remarkable. He had just tried to pass on what had been given to him—the grace, the patience, the radical belief that people mattered more than productivity.

But listening to them, he began to understand something. The gifts you give away don't disappear. They multiply. They echo forward into lives you'll never see, changing things in ways you'll never know.

That was the real retirement plan, he realized. Not a pension. Not a 401(k). But the legacy of grace, passed from hand to hand, life to life, generation to generation.

At noon, there was a gathering in the gardens.

Elena was there, holding his hand, her hair silver now but her eyes still the same—warm, wise, and full of a love that had only deepened with time. Grace and David stood nearby with their own families. Adam's grandchildren ran through the grass, laughing, oblivious to the significance of the day.

His mother was gone now—she'd passed five years ago, peacefully, in her sleep—but Adam could feel her presence somehow. Her prayers had carried him further than he'd ever know.

Joshua stood at the front of the gathering, looking exactly as he always had—ageless, calm, that quiet joy in his eyes.

"Forty years ago," Joshua said, "a young man walked out of a glass tower and into our lobby. He was broken. He was ashamed. He didn't believe he deserved to be here." He smiled at Adam. "He was wrong about that last part."

Soft laughter rippled through the crowd.

"Adam Cole has been many things in his time here," Joshua continued. "Analyst. Director. Vice president. Mentor. Friend. But more than any title, he has been faithful. Day after day, year after year, he showed up. He did the work. He loved the people in front of him. That's not glamorous. It's not the stuff of headlines. But it's the stuff of a life well lived."

Joshua raised his glass higher. "To Adam. For forty years of faithfulness. And for what comes next."

Everyone drank. Adam wiped his eyes, not bothering to hide the tears. Elena squeezed his hand.

The afternoon passed in a blur of handshakes and hugs. By four o'clock, the crowd had thinned, and Adam found himself alone in his office one last time.

He looked around at the space that had been his for so many years. The desk, the chair, the view of the gardens. He'd made decisions here that affected hundreds of lives. He'd had conversations that changed the trajectory of careers. He'd prayed here, wept here, and laughed here.

And now it was time to let it go.

He gathered the few personal items he wanted to keep—the photo, the drawing, the baseball, the stone. The rest could stay. Someone else would sit at this desk soon, would look out at these gardens, and would carry on the work. The mission was bigger than any one person. That was the point.

He thought of Marcus Webb—the warning he'd given Adam all those years ago in the Fyre Inc. elevator. *I don't know who I am without it anymore.* Marcus had been afraid of this moment. Afraid that without the job, the title, the identity, there would be nothing left.

But Adam wasn't afraid. He knew who he was—not because of what he'd done, but because of whose he was. His identity had never been in the work. It had been in the One who gave it.

He turned off the light, stepped into the hallway, and closed the door behind him.

Elena was waiting in the lobby, her coat over her arm. "Ready?"

Adam nodded. "Ready."

They walked out together, hand in hand, into the late afternoon sunlight. The gardens were quiet now, the celebration

CHAPTER SEVENTEEN

over, the day winding down. A few birds sang in the trees. The old brick building glowed behind them.

At the car, Adam paused and looked back one more time.

He thought about the young man who had arrived here forty years ago—desperate, broken, barely alive. He thought about everything that had happened since. The healing. The growth. The countless gifts of grace.

He'd come here with nothing—nothing but a willingness to accept what he couldn't earn. And he was leaving with everything that mattered.

"Thank you," he whispered. To the building. To the gardens. To the Father he couldn't see but had never stopped trusting.

Then he got in the car, and he and Elena drove home, into whatever came next.

Chapter Eighteen

COMING HOME

The invitation came three months after Adam's retirement. It arrived in an envelope—cream-colored, heavy stock, his name written on the front in handwriting he recognized immediately. The Father's handwriting. The same hand that had written *We're glad you're finally here* forty years ago.

Adam opened it at the kitchen table, Elena beside him, morning light streaming through the windows of the home they'd built together.

Inside was a single card. The message was brief:

> *Dear Adam,*
> *It's time to come home.*
> *There's a place prepared for you—*
> *there always has been.*
> *Joshua will come for you.*
>   *—The Father*

Adam read it twice. Then he set it down and looked at Elena.

She was crying—not with grief, but with something more complicated. Joy and sorrow, woven together. The tears of someone who understood what was being offered and what it would cost.

"How long?" she asked.

Adam shook his head. "I don't know. The letter doesn't say."

Elena took his hand—the same hand she'd held at their wedding, at the births of their children, through every hard season and every joy. "Then we'll make the most of the time we have. We always have."

The weeks that followed were ordinary and sacred.

Adam spent time with Grace and her family, watching his grandchildren play and listening to his daughter talk about her students. He spent time with David, now a physician with gray at his temples, and marveled at the man his son had become. He sat on the porch with Elena in the evenings, watching the sun set, talking about everything and nothing.

He wasn't afraid. That surprised him. He had always thought he would be afraid when this moment came. But instead, he felt something like anticipation—the way you feel before a long-awaited reunion, a homecoming you've been traveling toward your whole life.

He thought about his father, gone now for twenty-five years. He thought about his mother, her gentle prayers, her unshakeable faith. He thought about all the people who had gone before him—and he realized, with a quiet certainty, that he would see them again.

The Father had said there was a place prepared. Adam believed him. He had spent forty years learning to trust that voice, and it had never once led him wrong.

Joshua came on a Tuesday morning in early spring.

Adam was sitting on the porch, a cup of coffee in his hands, watching the birds at the feeder Elena had hung years ago. The morning was cool and bright, the kind of day that made you grateful simply to be alive.

He looked up and Joshua was there, walking across the lawn, unhurried as always. He looked exactly as he had on the loading

CHAPTER EIGHTEEN

dock forty years ago. Exactly as he had every day since. Time didn't seem to touch him the way it touched everyone else.

"Adam." Joshua climbed the porch steps and sat in the chair beside him. "How are you?"

Adam smiled. "Ready, I think. As ready as anyone can be."

Joshua nodded. He didn't rush. He never did. They sat together for a while, watching the birds, listening to the morning sounds of the world waking up.

"Do you remember," Joshua said, "the first time we met? In that conference room, when you came to interview?"

Adam laughed softly. "I remember thinking you were the strangest CEO I'd ever met. You asked me what I wanted my life to be about."

"You said you wanted to be successful."

"I did." Adam shook his head at his younger self. "I had no idea what that word meant."

"And now?"

Adam was quiet for a moment. He thought about his life—the choices he'd made, the roads he'd walked, the people he'd loved. He thought about the young man who had chased success and found only emptiness, and the older man who had surrendered everything and found everything that mattered.

"Now I know," he said. "Success isn't something you achieve. It's someone you become. It's the person you are when no one's watching, the love you give when there's nothing to gain, the faithfulness that compounds over a lifetime." He looked at Joshua. "You tried to tell me that, all those years ago. I wasn't ready to hear it."

"You heard it eventually. That's what matters." Joshua stood and extended his hand. "Are you ready to go?"

Adam looked at the hand—the same hand that had been offered on a loading dock, in a coffee shop, in a lobby. The hand that had never stopped reaching for him.

"One moment," he said. "There's someone I need to say goodbye to."

Elena was in the garden, kneeling among the flowers she'd planted decades ago. She looked up as Adam approached, and he saw that she already knew. She always knew.

He knelt beside her in the soft earth, taking her hands in his.

"It's time," he said.

She nodded, tears streaming down her face, but she was smiling too. "I know. I've known since this morning."

"Elena—"

"Don't." She touched his face, the way she had a thousand times before. "Don't apologize. Don't make promises. Just know that you gave me the most beautiful life. And I'll be right behind you. The Father promised."

Adam pulled her close and held her—held her the way he had on their wedding day, the way he had through every storm and every sunrise. He breathed in the scent of her, memorized the feel of her in his arms, and let the love he felt say what words could not.

"I'll wait for you," he whispered. "However long it takes. I'll be there when you come home."

She kissed him—one last kiss, tender and fierce—and then she let him go.

"Go," she said. "The Father's waiting."

Adam walked back to the porch where Joshua waited.

He didn't look back. He didn't need to. Everything he was leaving behind would be there when Elena arrived, and everything that truly mattered was going with him.

He took Joshua's hand.

"Where are we going?" he asked.

Joshua smiled—that warm, unhurried smile that had never changed in forty years.

"Home," he said. "The real one. The one that's been waiting for you since before you were born."

They stepped off the porch together, and the world around them began to change. The colors deepened. The light grew

CHAPTER EIGHTEEN

warmer, richer, more alive. The air itself seemed to hum with something Adam couldn't name—something that felt like joy distilled, like love made visible.

And then Adam saw it.

Ahead of them, through what had been his front yard and was now something else entirely, stood a building. Not the glass tower of Fyre Inc., cold and sharp. Not even the brick warmth of Light Co., beloved as it was. This was something beyond both—a structure of light and stone, ancient and new, vast and somehow intimate. It rose against a sky more blue than any Adam had ever seen, and every window blazed with welcome.

And standing at the entrance, arms open wide, was the Father.

He looked different here—more himself, somehow, as if everything Adam had seen before had been a shadow of this reality. His face was radiant with joy, and when he spoke, his voice was like thunder and a whisper all at once.

"Adam."

One word. His name. But in that word was everything—every prayer answered, every wound healed, every longing fulfilled. In that word was the sum of forty years of faithfulness and an eternity of love that had never, not for one moment, let him go.

Adam ran.

He ran like a child, like a son, like a man who had finally, after a lifetime of journeying, come home. The Father caught him in an embrace that was stronger than death, warmer than the sun, and deeper than any love Adam had ever known.

"Welcome home," the Father said. "Well done, good and faithful one. Enter into your rest."

And Adam, who had once been dead and was now more alive than he had ever been, wept with joy.

Later—though time meant something different here—Adam stood at a window in his new home, looking out at a landscape he was only beginning to understand.

Everything was more real here. More solid. More alive. The colors were colors he'd never seen before. The air was sweet with something that smelled like every good memory he'd ever had, distilled into a single breath. And the peace—the peace was like nothing he'd ever experienced. Not the absence of trouble, but the presence of something—Someone—that made trouble impossible to imagine.

Joshua stood beside him.

"It's a lot to take in," Joshua said.

Adam laughed—a real laugh, free and full, the laugh of a man with nothing left to fear. "That's an understatement." He turned to look at Joshua. "All those years—on the loading dock, in the coffee shop, walking out of Fyre Inc.—you were preparing me for this, weren't you?"

"We were preparing you for everything," Joshua said. "The work at Light Co. The family you built. The people you loved. And yes—this. It was always leading here."

"Why?" Adam asked. The question he'd asked so many times before. "Why me? Why any of this?"

Joshua smiled. The same smile. Always the same.

"Because you were worth it," he said. "You were always worth it. Not because of what you did or didn't do. But because you are loved. You have always been loved. And you will be loved forever."

Adam looked out at the endless beauty before him—the landscape of eternity, the home he'd been made for.

He thought about the young man he'd been, standing in that empty apartment with two letters, dreaming of success. He thought about the broken man on the loading dock, whispering *Help* into the darkness. He thought about the decades of faithfulness, the ordinary miracles, and the grace upon grace upon grace.

And he understood, finally, what it had all been for.

Not the corner office. Not the title. Not the success he'd once chased with such desperate hunger.

CHAPTER EIGHTEEN

This. This moment. This place. This eternal belonging in the presence of the One who had loved him before time began and would love him after time ended.

He had been dead, and he was alive.

He had been lost, and he was found.

He had been far away, and now—finally, fully, forever—he was home.

Afterword

The story you've just read is a parable.

Adam Cole isn't a real person, and Fyre Inc. isn't a real company. But the story Adam lives—the journey from death to life, from slavery to freedom, from condemnation to grace—is the truest story ever told. It's your story. It's mine. And it comes from a passage in the Bible that has changed countless lives for two thousand years.

I want to show you where this story came from—and more importantly, what it means for you.

In the New Testament, the apostle Paul wrote a letter to the church in Ephesus. In the second chapter, he described the human condition—and God's response to it—in words that echo across the centuries:

> *And you were dead in the trespasses and sins in which you once walked, following the course of this world, following the prince of the power of the air, the spirit that is now at work in the sons of disobedience—among whom we all once lived in the passions of our flesh, carrying out the desires of the body and the mind, and were by nature children of wrath, like the rest of mankind.*

> *But God, being rich in mercy, because of the great love with which he loved us, even when we were dead in our trespasses, made us alive together with Christ—by grace you have been saved—and raised us up with him and seated us with him in the heavenly places in Christ Jesus, so that in the coming ages he might show the immeasurable riches of his grace in kindness toward us in Christ Jesus.*
>
> *For by grace you have been saved through faith. And this is not your own doing; it is the gift of God, not a result of works, so that no one may boast. For we are his workmanship, created in Christ Jesus for good works, which God prepared beforehand, that we should walk in them.*
>
> EPHESIANS 2:1–10

Every element of Adam's story was drawn from these ten verses. Let me show you how.

"You were dead in the trespasses and sins in which you once walked."
Adam at Fyre Inc. was successful by every worldly measure—yet he was spiritually dead. The panic attacks, the sleepless nights, the hollow man staring back from the mirror—this was the portrait of a soul separated from God. He was walking, talking, and achieving, but he was not truly alive.

The Bible teaches that this is the natural state of every human being. We are separated from God because of sin—the decisions we have made that violated our Father's loving will for us. We may look alive on the outside, but spiritually, we are dead. And dead people cannot save themselves.

"Following the course of this world, following the prince of the power of the air."
Lucian Fyre represents Satan—the enemy of our souls. His name combines "Lucifer" and "fire," hinting at his true identity. Like Satan, Lucian was charming, attractive, and persuasive. He promised Adam success, significance, and belonging. "You

belong with us," he wrote—the same lie the enemy whispers to every human heart.

The glass tower of Fyre Inc. represents the world's system—the values, priorities, and promises that pull us away from God. It glitters. It impresses. It makes grand promises. But it leads only to bondage and death.

Notice that Adam chose this path. No one forced him. He walked into the tower with his eyes wide open, seduced by promises of greatness. This is how sin works—it presents itself as freedom while forging our chains.

"Among whom we all once lived in the passions of our flesh."
Adam's descent at Fyre Inc. followed the pattern of all sin. It started small—a compromise here, a rationalization there. "Every firm does it," Claire told him. And step by step, he became someone he never intended to be.

The betrayal of Daniel was his rock bottom—the moment he saw clearly what he had become. He had sacrificed another person to protect himself. He had become the very thing he once despised.

This is the trajectory of sin in every human life. We don't fall all at once. We drift, one small choice at a time, until we look up and can't see the shore.

"But God, being rich in mercy, because of the great love with which he loved us."
These two words—"But God"—are the turning point of the passage and the turning point of the story. Adam was dead, enslaved, and hopeless. *But God.*

Joshua represents Jesus Christ—the Son sent by the Father to seek and save the lost. His name is the English form of the Hebrew "Yeshua," which is the same name as Jesus. Throughout the story, Joshua displays the character of Christ: patient, pursuing, present in the darkest moments, offering grace without condition.

Joshua found Adam on the loading dock—not in a church, not in a holy place, but in the rubble of his broken life. That's where Jesus meets us too. He doesn't wait for us to clean ourselves up. He comes to us where we are.

"Even when we were dead in our trespasses, made us alive together with Christ."

Adam's first morning at Light Co.—when he woke without dread, noticed the birds singing, and felt something stir in his chest that he almost didn't recognize—this was resurrection. He had been dead, and now he was alive.

This is what happens when a person trusts in Jesus. The Bible calls it being born again—a spiritual resurrection, a new life that begins not when we die physically, but the moment we put our faith in Christ, repent, and are baptized. The old self passes away. Everything becomes new.

"By grace you have been saved through faith. And this is not your own doing; it is the gift of God, not a result of works."

This is the heart of the gospel, and it's the heart of Adam's story.

Adam could not save himself. The debt was too great—the clawbacks, the non-compete, the financial penalties. He was trapped. No amount of effort could free him.

But Joshua paid it all. "My Father can cover all of it," he said. "Every dollar. Every clause. Every threat." The debt wasn't ignored or dismissed—it was paid in full by someone else.

This is exactly what Jesus did for us. The Bible teaches that the penalty for sin is death—eternal separation from God. We owe a debt we cannot pay. But Jesus, the sinless Son of God, went to the cross and paid it for us. He absorbed the penalty. He took what we deserved.

And here is the astonishing part: this gift is *free*. Adam didn't earn it. He couldn't earn it. All he had to do was accept it—to trust Joshua's word, walk out of Fyre Inc., and begin a new life.

AFTERWORD

Grace means getting what we don't deserve. Mercy means not getting what we do deserve. In Jesus, we receive both.

"For we are his workmanship, created in Christ Jesus for good works, which God prepared beforehand."
Adam's years at Light Co. weren't about earning his salvation—that was already secured. They were about becoming who he was made to be. The mentoring, the meaningful work, the love he poured into others—this was the fruit of grace, not the price of it.

The Father told him: "I didn't bring you here to talk about who you were. I brought you here to talk about who you're becoming."

When we trust in Jesus, we are saved for good works, not by them. God has a purpose for every life—work prepared in advance for us to do. Not to earn his love, but because we already have it.

"Raised us up with him and seated us with him in the heavenly places."
The final chapter of Adam's story—his homecoming, his entrance into the Father's house—represents the ultimate promise of the gospel: eternal life with God.

The Father's embrace. The words "Well done, good and faithful one." The home prepared since before time began. This is what awaits everyone who puts their trust in Jesus.

Heaven is not a reward for good behavior. It is the destination grace has always been leading toward—the place where faith becomes sight, where the presence of God we've tasted in this life becomes our eternal reality.

Now I want to speak directly to you.

Perhaps you picked up this book because you liked the cover, or someone recommended it, or you were curious about the premise. But I don't believe in accidents. I believe you're reading these words right now because God is pursuing you—the same way Joshua pursued Adam.

Maybe you recognize yourself in Adam's story. Maybe you've been climbing a ladder that's leaning against the wrong wall. Maybe you've made compromises you're not proud of. Maybe you feel trapped—by success, by failure, by choices you can't undo.

Or maybe you're doing fine by the world's standards, but something is missing. A restlessness you can't name. A hunger that success hasn't satisfied. A quiet voice asking, *Is this all there is?*

Here is the good news: the offer is still open.

Jesus Christ, the Son of God, came to earth two thousand years ago. He lived a perfect life. He died on a cross, taking the punishment for your sins and mine. Three days later, he rose from the dead, conquering death and opening the way to eternal life.

And now he stands at the door of your heart, offering you the same thing Joshua offered Adam: freedom. Forgiveness. A new life. A place at the Father's table.

You cannot earn this. You cannot be good enough to deserve it. That's the point. It's a gift—received by grace, through faith.

So how do you receive it?

Believe. Trust that Jesus is who he claimed to be—the Son of God, the Savior of the world. Believe that his death paid your debt in full. Believe that his resurrection guarantees your own. "If you confess with your mouth that Jesus is Lord and believe in your heart that God raised him from the dead, you will be saved" (Romans 10:9).

Repent. Turn away from your old life—the sins, the selfishness, the pursuit of empty things. Repentance isn't just feeling sorry; it's a change of direction. It's walking out of Fyre Inc. and never looking back. "Repent and turn to God, performing deeds in keeping with your repentance" (Acts 26:20).

Be baptized. When you go under the water, you identify with Christ's death—the old self, buried. When you come up,

AFTERWORD

you identify with his resurrection—the new self, raised to life. "Repent and be baptized every one of you in the name of Jesus Christ for the forgiveness of your sins, and you will receive the gift of the Holy Spirit" (Acts 2:38).

This is how you walk out of Fyre Inc. This is how you accept the offer that has been waiting for you all along.

Adam thought he had waited too long. He thought he had done too much, fallen too far, accumulated too much debt. He thought grace like this couldn't possibly be for someone like him.

He was wrong.

And if you're thinking the same thing right now—that you've waited too long, done too much, fallen too far—you're wrong too.

The offer is still open. It has never closed. Jesus is standing at the door, the same way Joshua stood in that lobby, waiting to walk out with you.

All you have to do is say yes.

Welcome to Light Co.

Welcome home.

"The offer will remain open. Whenever you're ready. If you find yourself lost—just call. I'll come find you."

www.ingramcontent.com/pod-product-compliance
Lightning Source LLC
LaVergne TN
LVHW012000070526
838202LV00054B/4988